THE CANON CODE:

Freud, C. S. Lewis, Et Al.

Solve *The Mystery Of Edwin Drood*

REVISED EDITION

Jon Gegenheimer

In Memoriam
Cary D. Livingston
1950-2021

Published in the United States of America

ISBN 979-8-9924880-2-9 (SC)

ISBN 979-8-9924880-3-6 (HC)

For Book Rights Adaption and other Rights Permission.
Call us at toll-free **601-914-6178**.

Table of Contents

INTRODUCTION

On 9 June 1870, Charles Dickens died at Gad's Hill Place, the home he loved. Four days later at Westminster Abbey, the son of Kent became part of the dust of London. *The Mystery of Edwin Drood* lay on his desk, half-finished on paper but completely thought out. Over the years, many have proposed clumsy, speculative theories about how his last novel would end. They ignore the fundamental maxim from Sherlock Holmes: "It is a capital mistake to theorize in advance of the facts. Insensibly, one begins to twist facts to suit theories, instead of theories to suit facts."

In 1925, Sigmund Freud and three Oxford academics, including C. S. Lewis, set out to determine what actually happened to the young man who inexplicably disappeared at an isolated weir near Rochester, England on Christmas morning 1860. They travel from Oxford to Rochester to London and retrace the steps of *Drood*'s pivotal characters. Along the way, Freud calls on his Holmesian imagination and deductive-reasoning skills to identify clues, find tangible evidence, connect the dots, and arrange all the pieces to the puzzle. He sees a possibility no one ever thought of; and, unlike his feckless forerunners, the Austrian maven solves the mystery and brings *Drood* to its *true* conclusion, just as Dickens had contemplated.

The setting is a remote English town – a 'speck on the globe' that epitomizes Western civilization, a culture that is at once flawed and virtuous. Dickens's alluring story captures the essence of the human experience – the impact of society on those subject to its norms, mores, and laws. *Edwin Drood* is about (a) the eternal tug-of-war between good and evil; (b) cultural assimilation; (c) the curse of opium; (d) imprisonment; (e) faith; (f) redemption; and something else, to be revealed at the appropriate time.

The *rest* of *Drood*, which did not make it to paper until 1981, confirms the unbounded capacity of literature's man for all seasons – a man for all times, especially today, a troublous period unlike any the world has ever seen.

PROLOGUE

I

I am Chiswell Bucktrout, born 16 November 1898 in London to Robin Bucktrout, a respected barrister associated with Gray's Inn,[1] and Lucinda Chiswell, a popular playwright who introduced me to the engaging world of Victorian literature. I have no middle name, and my parents could not bring themselves to call me either Chiswell or 'Chis'. So, they rewarded me with the moniker 'Buck'.

Their combined incomes enabled our family of three to live in a fashionable townhouse in Curzon Street, Mayfair. I received my preparatory education at prestigious Westminster School and moved on to Magdalen College, Oxford, to earn undergraduate, graduate, and doctoral degrees in English literature. In 1925, I became a teaching fellow[2] at my alma mater.

II

My favourite Oxford professor was Cambridge-educated Haywood Townes Chambers Jr., the world's leading expert on Charles

---

[1] Gray's Inn is one of the four Inns of Court (bar associations for barristers and judges) in London.

[2] A 'teaching fellow' is a junior faculty member who lectures and often is engaged in research.

Dickens. Though three-eighths English and five-eighths Indian, he was the quintessential 'Brit'.

In 1922, I enrolled in his Dickens proseminar: 'What *Really* Happened to Edwin Drood?' I was intimately familiar with *The Mystery of Edwin Drood* – left half-done when Dickens died on 9 June 1870.

III

Edwin Drood mysteriously disappeared near the river in the town that Dickens named Cloisterham. No corpse was ever found. Only a watch and chain, ensnared on a weir, and a stick-pin, resting securely and unobtrusively at the water's edge, were recovered. Some pundits have said that young Drood was murdered. Others argued that he drowned accidentally or survived a murder attempt and reappeared, disguised, to unveil his attacker. None of the numerous proposed 'theories' satisfied Professor Chambers, who never offered his own hypothesis. Instead, he issued a final assignment: 'Solve *The Mystery of Edwin Drood.*'

I remember his instructions exactly: "Your paper shall not exceed 150 pages – typewritten, double-spaced, on standard-size bond paper, with 2½ centimeter margins all-round. Begin your essay with a concise summary of Dickens's unfinished story. Do *not* write a mere narrative/dialogue continuation of the novel. Rather, take what Dickens gave us and identify clues. Connect the dots and draw your fact-based conclusion(s) about Edwin Drood's fate." I titled my 125-page paper

'Edwin Drood Remains a Mystery'. I had decided that the puzzle is insoluble due to the lack of indispensable clues. For the next three years, I wrestled with doubt about my 'cop-out' conclusion.

IV

<u>10 December 1925</u>.

On a damp December afternoon, I attended, as Professor Chambers's guest, a lecture by Sigmund Freud at Trinity College, Oxford. Freud's topic was '*The Mystery of Edwin Drood*: Dickens as Psychologist'.

Our eager host introduced the celebrated Austrian:

> Greetings! I am Haywood Townes Chambers Jr., professor of English Literature at Magdalen College. Some of you may see me as *the* expert on the life and works of Charles Dickens. I'm not so sure I deserve that distinction.
>
> I am pleased to introduce the devoted Dickensian who has based some of his psychoanalytic theories on the complex personalities of various Dickens characters. Our speaker's address focuses on the synergistic interaction of (a) the insightful Victorian writer's creations

and (b) *his own* modern, revolutionary ideas about the human personality.

With us today is a rare philosopher/empiricist, who I predict will be ranked, alongside Einstein, atop the list of the 20th century's most influential leaders in the scientific arena.

Distinguished guests, please greet the world's foremost behavioural analyst – the creator of psychoanalysis, Dr. Sigmund Freud.

For ninety minutes, the man of the hour talked about Dickens's metaphysical grasp of human nature and the human psyche. According to Dr. Freud, the greatness of Dickens lay in his unique ability to humanize aberrant behaviour, that is, show it as a function of human frailty, misguided motives, or downright evil. The perceptive scientist pointed to specific sections in the *Drood* dialogue as genuine lessons in psychoanalysis. He explained that Dickens was already 'Freudian' when he (Freud) was a child, oblivious to the id-ego-superego dynamic – the structural model of the mind he developed in 1923.

After the lecture, Professor Chambers and I sauntered to the Eagle & Child to meet C. S. Lewis,[3] like me, a hopeful, dedicated

---

[3] Clive Staples Lewis (1898-1963) liked his childhood nickname, 'Jack', derived from 'Jacksie', his dog, run over and killed when his master was only four. For a while, he would answer only to 'Jacksie'; but he gradually accepted 'Jack', by which he was

teaching fellow at Magdalen College. We joined him at his corner spot in the Rabbit Room, where the three of us talked over claret about Freud's performance. [At Chambers's request, C. S. had arranged Freud's stay at the nearby Macdonald Randolph Hotel.]

"C. S., why didn't you invite Dr. Freud to join us?"

"Don't be so irritable, Buck. I'm asking Haywood and you to join Freud and me at dinner this evening at the Randolph, where you can talk to him for as long as he will listen."

"Terrific! I have a proposal for him."

"What's that?"

"I'll ask him to help me solve *The Mystery of Edwin Drood*."

"Freud the detective!"

"Freud is Holmes, and I am Watson."

"My dear Bucktrout, if Dr. Freud is Holmes; and you are Watson, *you* will assist *him*."

"Aah, C. S. Lewis, the observant philosopher. You are correct. Should he accept my offer, the good doctor will drive the coach; and, as they used to say in the American Wild West, I will ride shotgun."

---

known to friends and family for the duration of his life. Most of his academic associates and the general public knew him as and called him 'C. S.'.

Lewis became a famed British writer, philosopher, lay theologian, and Christian apologist. He taught English literature and philosophy at the Universities of Oxford and Cambridge.

My old professor excitedly asked: "May I come along for the ride? I want to observe Freud and you as you try to tackle the *Drood* conundrum."

"Of course," I replied. "After all, Haywood, *you* are the Dickens expert."

Chiswell Bucktrout
Oxford, ENG[4]

---

[4] On 2 January 1981, fifty-plus years after Sigmund Freud, Haywood Chambers Jr., C. S. Lewis, and I left Westminster Abbey, I began to write the following story, an odyssey that had started in the Macdonald Randolph Hotel and ended at the grave of the Victorian era's noblest man of letters.

CHAPTER 1

A SUMMARY OF WHAT WE HAVE

It is my business to know what other people don't know.

Sherlock Holmes
"The Adventure of the Blue Carbuncle"

It is a capital mistake to theorize in advance of the facts. Insensibly, one begins to twist facts to suit theories, instead of theories to suit facts.

Sherlock Holmes
"A Scandal in Bohemia"

10 December 1925 (continued).

I

C. S. had reserved a cozy, private dining room adjoining the Randolph's Morse Bar. Professor Chambers and I arrived at 18:45, tastefully early for our 19:00 dinner engagement. We ordered two clarets and stood at the bar.

At 18:55, my teaching-fellow cohort and a sprightly, slim, meditative gentleman of average height, who appeared no older than his 69 years, approached us.

Freud's thinning grey hair was neatly combed, precisely parted on the left side, and carefully trimmed above the ears. I surmised that, at the back, it was no farther than two and a half centimetres from his starched collar, tied with an understated, royal blue cravat. His nicely groomed, modest mustache and beard were a lighter grey than his hair. He wore a three-piece dark flannel suit, complemented by a gold watch and its chain, which meandered from the middle button of his vest to the watch in its left pocket.

Chambers and I extended our hands. As Freud shook mine, I noticed the warmth in his dark eyes – deep-set orbs, perfectly positioned above his aquiline nose. I thought, *This chap is not tall, yet he is a giant amongst men.*

C. S. was a savvy host. Four sparkling stem glasses awaited us on the private dining room's only table, covered in white cloth and accoutred with a crystal vase holding pink roses. A bottle of White Bordeaux rested in a silver cooler near the table. We took our seats, and the waiter made the first pours.

Freud, a serious man of business, eschewed small talk.

"Dr. Bucktrout, C. S. said you feel obligated to unriddle the *Drood* mystery; and you want me to lead the way. When shall we start?" [Freud's accent was rather heavy, but his English was clear and fluent.]

"You accept my proposal?"

"By all means. I can't wait to play a role in your ambitious project. I have read all the fatuous theories of how the novel ends. What claptrap!"

"Where and when do we begin, Dr. Freud?"

"May I call you Buck?"

"I insist that you do."

"And, I'm Sig."

"Sig it is! Now, where do we go from here?"

"We *begin* here, in this lovely room, by analysing what Dickens has left for us."

"You apparently agree with my old professor [I motioned towards Chambers], who so instructed us for the final paper in his proseminar. He was emphatic: '… Take what Dickens gave us and identify clues ... Draw fact-based conclusions about Edwin Drood's fate.'

"I have regretted my lackluster solution. I didn't strive hard enough to find clues and piece them together. I am determined to redeem myself."

Chambers: "It's too late to up your grade, Buck."

C. S was amused.

"Hear, hear! Let's drink to that!"

II

Sometimes presumptuous, but never arrogantly so, C. S. had decided, sua sponte, on the meal: tomato soup, onion and beet salad, steak and kidney pudding, and raisin-nut oat cakes topped with clotted cream.

The soup arrived, and Sigmund Freud spoke:

A.

"The starting point is the title itself: *The* Mystery *of Edwin* Drood. Notice my emphasis on 'mystery', which has various synonyms: 'riddle, enigma, thriller, mind-boggler, puzzle, stumper', and so on. The *definitions* of 'mystery' are disparate: 'anything that is *kept secret or remains unexplained or unknown*; a novel or other form of story that remains puzzlingly unsettled *until the very end*.' Did Dickens intend to leave the young man's fate, after he vanished into thin air, unknown? Will his corpse surface and point to the murderer? Did he commit suicide? Did he, Houdini-like,[5] escape death and return to Cloisterham as someone else to expose his attacker? Those inquiries, amongst others, comprise the mystery. We are left hanging at the story's midpoint."

"Sig, do you think Dickens would have left the mystery unresolved?"

---

[5] Harry Houdini (1874-1926) was an American illusionist and stunt man, famous for his amazing escape acts.

"Buck, as you and Professor Chambers know, Dickens, like most Victorian writers, would never expect his readers to wrestle with uncertainty. I think he meant to tell us (a) what actually happened to Drood and (b) all the circumstances surrounding his fate – before, during, and after his disappearance.

"Two of Sherlock Holmes's aphorisms come to mind:

> 1. It is my business to know what other people don't know.

> 2. It is a capital mistake to theorize in advance of the facts. Insensibly, one begins to twist facts to suit theories, instead of theories to suit facts.

"There are unknown things – actual *facts* that we need to unveil before we can disentangle the *Drood* knot. We must gather and arrange *all* the facts, which I shall call data points. Then, we can formulate our conclusions about the outcome. We must curb our passion and exercise reason based on cold, hard *facts*. Our task is not to continue the story in pure-novel format. It is to line up the clues and solve the problem, just as Haywood's proseminar instructions required.

"Is it alright to call you Haywood, Professor?"

"Of course! I prefer that you *do*, Sig."

My cohort sang out.

"Well, although I'm C. S., I think you all will call me 'Jack' before too long."

Freud: "Jack?"

"It's a long story. I'll tell you how I was blessed with that nickname after we complete our assignment."

Freud resumes: "Well, let's begin ...

"Those who have pretended to figure out *Drood* did not heed Holmes. They acted on pure impulse and manufactured facts to support rank conjecture. Few, if any, of the prognosticators actually walked the streets of 'Cloisterham'. *We* shall do just that and follow the paths of the main characters. We shall become detectives. We shall *not* assume the roles of donnish speculators.

"You probably noticed I also stressed the 'Drood' name. Why did Dickens choose that odd surname? Is 'Drood' an adaptation of 'Druid' – the ancient Celtic priest and wizard who had magical qualities? Is there something paranormal about this fellow?

"Before we go to 'Cloisterham', which we know is in fact Rochester, and on to London, we should first recapitulate and explicate what we know."

A second bottle of White Bordeaux; the salad; hot, stone-ground brown bread; and butter arrived. Freud had some wine; drew lightly on his inoffensive cigar; took out his copious notes; and set about summarizing *Edwin Drood* at its halfway point.

B.

"I will cite a few passages from the story: dialogue, descriptive phrases and sentences, diary entries, and letters. They are Dickens's work and require attribution.[6]

"*Drood* begins as its central figure, John 'Jack' Jasper, awakens from a restless dream. He's in a dingy, smoggy room at one of London's infamous East End opium dens. The dream was about a Turkish sultan, a despot who reveled in public execution, through which he maintained absolute control over his fear-stricken subjects.

"One of the dream's arresting features was an ominous spike rising from a cathedral tower. I see the spike as a metaphor for violence and eroticism. I contend that every dream is a physical structure that has a meaning attributable to one's mental process in waking life.

"Jasper is only twenty-six, but he appears much older. Opium no doubt has aged him prematurely and warped his personality – as we soon shall see.

"In the room with Jasper are three other opium smokers: a 'Chinaman'; a witch-like woman, ostensibly the proprietrix; and a lascar. Jasper loathes these addicts. He sees himself in them, and he subconsciously loathes *himself*. After roughing up the 'Chinaman', he drags the lascar across the floor. When he is sufficiently sober, Jasper

---

[6] Throughout Freud's commentary, he cited dialogue and phrases from *The Mystery of Edwin Drood*. – marked in these pages with single quotation marks.

returns to Cloisterham to resume his putative role as the old town's tame, reticent cathedral choirmaster.

C.

"The next chapter introduces Reverend Septimus Crisparkle, Cloisterham Cathedral's mild-mannered, resolute minor canon. Dickens describes him as an 'early riser, good-natured, cheerful, social, boy-like, a good man' – the polar opposite of Jasper, a secretive, somber, schizophrenic who is prone to violence.

"Also appearing is Edwin Drood, Jasper's nephew and ward, whom he calls 'Ned'. Drood is a twenty-year-old apprentice engineer. He arrives in Cloisterham from London to visit Jasper and stay at his house. Ned had been for some time in Egypt, employed in the firm founded there by his late father. At Jasper's house, uncle and nephew talk about Ned's attractive, 17-year-old fiancée, Rosa Bud, whom he also will visit to discuss their future. After their marriage, the couple will move to Egypt, where Edwin will run the Egyptian engineering firm. Jasper has other ideas; he secretly wants Rosa as his own.

"There is a frivolous, amateurish painting of Rosa mounted on Jasper's wall. The artist is young Drood, who, at this stage of his life, is a shameless dilettante who doesn't respect his intended. The painting attests that he recklessly takes her for granted. He condescendingly calls her 'Miss Pussy'. Likewise, Rosa has little regard for *him*. Their marriage was fixed by their fathers, absent their concurrence; and they resent being played as pawns.

"Jasper tells his nephew that, contrary to what the locals believe, he hates his job and his pedestrian life in Cloisterham, which Dickens calls 'a drowsy, monotonous, silent city [whose] changes lie behind it'. Notably, he also says of the stagnant town: 'For sufficient reasons, which this narrator will unfold as it advances, a fictitious name must be bestowed upon the old cathedral town. Let it stand [for now] as Cloisterham.' The words 'for now' are *my* insertions. You will understand my add-on soon enough. Dickens's catching elucidation about Cloisterham is highly significant. I have a conditional theory of why he offers it. I say 'conditional' because we must remember Holmes's admonition: 'It is a capital mistake to theorize in advance of the facts.'

"Rosa lives and studies in Cloisterham at the Nuns' House, a girls' boarding school. Drood calls on her. They engage in puerile chitchat, which reveals their utter lack of commitment to each other.

D.

"In virtually all of his novels, Dickens often abruptly changes settings as he introduces new characters. In so doing, he thickens the plot and expands the theme. On the heels of Jasper, Crisparkle, Drood, and Rosa, he gives us the sententious boor, Luke Honeythunder, and his two wards – Neville and Helena Landless, whom he is bringing to be schooled by Crisparkle and the Nuns' House, respectively. They are twins from Ceylon, 'unusually handsome and very dark'. Dickens adds: '[T]here is something untamed about them, a certain air upon them of hunter and huntress [and at the same time] the [hunted] … beautiful, barbaric captives brought from wild tropical dominion.'

"Crisparkle asks Neville how Honeythunder became his guardian. Neville reveals that he and his sister know little about him. They had lived in Ceylon with their stepfather, who treated them horribly. Upon his death, they were awarded to Honeythunder.

"There is instructive dialogue between Crisparkle and Neville, a young man who proves to be mature and candid: 'My sister and I came to quarrel with you and leave. But, we [have come] to like you. You graciously received us and [have] treated us like no one else ever did.' Neville then says of his sister: 'She has come out of the disadvantages of our miserable life … as much better than I am – as that cathedral tower is higher than those chimneys … She is brave, a leader with the daring of a man. She planned our runaways from home …'

"The minor canon listens respectfully to his new pupil and responds forthrightly: 'I will not repay your confidence with a sermon … I will help you, but you must also help yourself … by seeking aid from Heaven.'

"That interesting interaction sheds a bright light on the Landless twins, who, like Jasper and Crisparkle, are crucial to plot and theme.

E.

"Shortly, Crisparkle and Neville witness a galling episode at Crisparkle's residence in Minor Canon Corner. Jasper is on the piano accompanying Rosa, his student, as she sings. Rosa loses her composure and cries. Helena is there with the frightened girl, whom she has befriended. She lays her on the sofa and comforts her. Jasper remains at the piano, creepily silent, as though nothing is wrong. Her hapless fiancé apathetically looks on.

"Helena accompanies Rosa to the Nuns' House, where they will become roommates. Rosa betrays her intense fear of Jasper: 'He terrifies me … he has made a slave of me … when I sing, he never moves his eyes from my lips …'

"Afterwards, Neville and Edwin get together at Jasper's house. An altercation erupts. Neville is attracted to Rosa and deplores Edwin's cavalier treatment of the person who should enjoy his respect. The argument intensifies, as Jasper watches with plotting eyes. He serves them wine spiked with opium, which exacerbates their mutual anger. Jasper adds more fuel to the fire: 'Neville, look at my nephew. He lounges so easily … the world is all before him … You and I are wretches … with no prospect but the tedious, unchanging round of this dull place.'

"The situation deteriorates further, as Edwin speaks insultingly of Neville's brown skin. Neville throws his wine goblet at him and retreats to Minor Canon Corner, where Crisparkle has him as his boarder. The minor canon confronts his pupil: 'You are not sober.' Neville sheepishly responds: 'I had a little to drink. It overcame me ... We quarreled ... He insulted me grossly ... and heated my tigerish blood.'

"At this juncture, Jasper's malevolence is glaringly obvious. He has succeeded in pitting Neville and Edwin against each other. He plans to spread the word about Neville's assault on his nephew. Jasper is stirring big trouble.

"Whispers of Neville's wild temper circulate. Crisparkle vehemently defends the swarthy Oriental youngster.

"He decides to jog to the river to seek spiritual refuge in 'the sweetening powers of Cloisterham Weir'. On the way, he chances upon Helena ... and Neville, who reveals his fondness for Rosa and his disdain for Edwin. The principled minor canon admonishes Neville and exclaims that he has no right to rag Edwin for his shabby treatment of her. He persuades him to strike a compromise and end the bitter dispute that began under John Jasper's roof.

"After the encounter at the river, the aspiring peacemaker asks Jasper to help him work out a truce. Jasper takes from his desk a book, his diary, and reads:

> Ned up and away. Light-hearted
> and unsuspicious as ever. He laughed
> when I cautioned him, and said he was as
> good a man as Neville Landless any day.

I told him that might be, but he was not as bad a man. He continued to make light of it, but I travelled with him as far as I could, and left him most unwillingly. I am unable to shake off these dark intangible presentiments of evil – if feelings founded upon staring facts are to be so called.[7]

"Crisparkle tries to quiet Jasper's concerns, which he doesn't yet realize are contrived to establish a false case against Neville for the murder of Edwin Drood. Unexpectedly, Jasper promises the minor canon that he will have his nephew write a peace-offering. A few days later, he produces a signed note:

> My Dear Jack,
>
> I am touched by your account of your interview with Mr. Crisparkle, whom I much respect and esteem. At once I openly say that I forgot myself on that occasion quite as much as Mr. Landless did, and that I wish that bygone to be a bygone, and all to be right again.

---

[7] From time to time during his review, Freud read passages from correspondence and diary entries as they appeared in the novel. They are double indented.

> Look here, dear old boy. Ask
> Mr. Landless to dinner on Christmas Eve
> (the better the day the better the deed),
> and let there be only we three, and let us
> shake hands all round there and then, and
> say no more about it.
>
> My dear Jack,
>
>> Ever your most affectionate,
>> Ned
>
> P.S. Love to Miss Pussy at the next music
> lesson.

"Crisparkle asks Jasper to acknowledge Drood's request and invite the antagonists to dinner on Christmas Eve, where they will shake hands and settle their differences.

"In the meantime, Drood calls on the London office of Rosa's guardian, Mr. Grewgious, a peripheral, though not insignificant character. The stern curator assails his visitor for his supercilious attitude toward Rosa: 'You mustn't make a plaything of a treasure.' He gives him the engagement ring that belonged to Rosa's mother. It was removed from her dead hand after she drowned. Grewgious tells his ward's grudging fiancé: 'If you have any doubts, bring the ring back to me.'

F.

"Dickens takes us directly to the next setting, the cathedral cemetery and crypt – with Jasper and Stony Durdles, the grave marker/stonemason, who knows more than anyone else about those desolate places. Nearby, they pass a mound of quick-lime, 'quick enough to eat your bones', said the seedy, creepy mason. I surmise that quick-lime is a metaphor that Dickens planned to furnish near the end of the story. Time will tell.

G.

"At Christmas recess, we see a change in Drood. The young man has a conscience, after all; and Grewgious pricked it. He visits Rosa. For the first time, they show mutual respect. There is no more child's play. During a mature, sobersided talk, they decide against marriage. Edwin will return the engagement ring to Grewgious.

H.

"Christmas Eve arrives. That afternoon, Neville meticulously straightens up his room, neatly packs some clothes into a knapsack, and gets out his iron-wood walking stick. He has planned a long hike, to begin on Christmas morning and last for a fortnight.

"Edwin spends the day alone and dejected, as he contritely recalls his inconsiderate treatment of Rosa. He sadly ponders his romantic attraction to Helena, who he believes is outside his reach.

"The Christmas Eve dinner-hour is fast approaching. On his way to Jasper's place, Edwin chances upon a menacing crone, staring at him through vacant eyes. He leans down and sees she is trembling, 'like Jack sometimes is', he thinks. She says she's from London and smokes opium. She adds: 'Be thankful your name isn't Ned. It is a threatened, dangerous name.' Well, we know that 'Ned' is Jasper's nickname for Edwin; and we can reasonably suspect that the choirmaster's unconscious utterances in the London opium den pointed to his plan to murder his nephew.

"Jasper, wearing his black silk scarf, is singing beautifully as he leads the Cloisterham choir at the Christmas Eve service. He's upbeat and composed, because his plan to murder his nephew, by strangling him with his scarf, has been finalised.

"The conniving choirmaster goes home, where he will host the dinner at which Neville and Edwin will end their discord. The friendly meal ends around midnight. The two young men make peace and go together, in amiable spirts, to the river to watch the storm that began as they enjoyed dinner.

"At mid-morning on Christmas, Jasper confronts the minor canon: 'Where is my nephew? He went down to the river last night with Mr. Neville to look at the storm and has not been back. Call Mr. Neville!'

I.

"By this time, Neville is leaving Cloisterham, carrying his knapsack and walking stick. He is stopped by eight men, who were following him. After a struggle, his captors return him to town.

"A hectic, around-the-clock search for Edwin Drood begins. Jasper, as much as anyone, wants the body to be found. It would be solid evidence of murder against Neville, and confirmation of death will enable Jasper to propose to Rosa. But, he learns from Grewgious that the young couple cancelled their engagement. Panic consumes him, as he thinks he killed his nephew for nothing.

"Crisparkle believes something sinister happened at the river. He soon returns there with other Drood hunters (Jasper is in plain sight amongst them), who begin a further exhaustive search of the immediate area. Nothing turns up after days of dredging the river's bottom and combing its banks.

"One day, the minor canon goes back alone to scour the site yet again. Volltreffer![8] He sees a gold watch and chain stranded on the weir, which crosses the tributary leading to the river. He swims to the weir and retrieves the watch and chain. Engraved on the back of the watch is 'E. D'. He thinks, *The body must be nearby*! He dives repeatedly into the restive, bone-numbing tributary in search of a submerged corpse. The intrepid clergyman finds only a stick-pin stuck

---

[8] The German word for 'Bingo' (as an exclamation); direct hit; bullseye.

in the mud beside the weir. His search ends when he can no longer withstand the water's bite.

"He takes the watch, chain, and pin to Mayor Sapsea, who sends for Jasper. The recovered items incriminate Neville, the last person seen with Drood. The mayor orders further digging at and around the weir. No remains are found. For the time being, Sapsea releases the suspect from custody. Later, the embattled young fellow from Ceylon will be charged with murder and jailed.

J.

"Six months pass. Crisparkle is now the Landless twins' legal guardian. He travels to London to visit Neville, free after the murder charge was dismissed. He is staying in a small suite at Staple('s) Inn,[9] where Grewgious has his chambers. Neville has boundless respect for his dutiful curator: 'If I were dying, I feel as if your touch would make my pulse beat again ...' At this point, Dickens has established Crisparkle's Jesus persona.

---

[9] The site of old Staple('s) Inn, on High Holborn Street in London, is near Gray's Inn and Lincoln's Inn, two of the Inns of Court. See note 1, supra. The other Inns are the Middle Temple and the Inner Temple. Staple's Inn was the last surviving Inn of Chancery, where barristers were trained until the early 19th century, when the Inns of Chancery gave way to the Inns of Court. Furnival's Inn, hereinafter mentioned, was another Inn of Chancery, older than Staple's Inn.

For some time, both of the former Chancery Inns remained as residences after the Inns of Court replaced them. Dickens lived at Furnival's Inn from 1834 to 1837. He began *The Pickwick Papers* (1837) whilst there.

"Enter Dick Datchery, a mysterious gent with abundant white hair. He has rented a place near Cloisterham Cathedral and intends to become a permanent resident. He asks Mayor Sapsea about Jasper: 'Is he the one who lost his nephew and devotes his life to avenging the loss?' I don't think Datchery will become a major player.

K.

"Dickens takes us to the Nuns' House, where Rosa receives an unwelcome visitor, John Jasper. She hasn't seen him since the evening before the disappearance – when he sang at the cathedral's Christmas Eve service. Jasper confesses to Rosa that he is madly in love with her. His loathsome manner confirms his neurotic, wicked, bestial obsession. Rosa overcomes her fear and sternly rejects her late voice instructor, who leaves, much as a frustrated predator retreats from its elusive prey. After this minacious encounter, Rosa fears that Jasper murdered Edwin. She sees Neville Landless as Jasper's scapegoat, set up to divert attention from the actual culprit.

"Rosa goes to London to pre-empt further intimidation by Jasper. She visits Grewgious at Staple's Inn. The Landless twins stay across the courtyard from him. Rosa tells her guardian about Jasper's crude advances. Grewgious arranges safe lodgings for her at nearby Furnival's Inn.

"The minor canon arrives in London to meet Grewgious, who informs him of Jasper's psychopathic advances toward Rosa. A new character, Mr. Tartar, is also boarding at Staple's Inn. He enters the conversation between Crisparkle and Grewgious. Tartar and Crisparkle immediately recognise each other. When they were schoolmates, Tartar saved Crisparkle from drowning. Will the man who rescued the future churchman from water's clawing hands help us find what's behind the baffling disappearance of Edwin Drood? I think he might.

"Jasper and Crisparkle soon begin to meet daily at Cloisterham Cathedral. Finally, Jasper reveals a startling diary account – dominated by the following words:

Neville killed Edwin, and I will avenge my nephew's death.

"Jasper returns to the London opium den, where he meets its drug-addicted owner, Princess Puffer. The colloquy between those devilish creatures is the kind of interaction one sees when a psychoanalyst engages his hypnotised patient. As Jasper surrenders to the soporific, mesmerising influence of opium, the scheming hag learns of his perfected plot to strangle his nephew, dump him into the river, and implicate Neville. She follows Jasper to Cloisterham. On her arrival, she stumbles upon Datchery, who informs her that Jasper is the cathedral choirmaster.

"Puffer plans to blackmail Jasper by threatening to expose his 'admission' as expressed in his drug-induced utterances in the opium den. She goes to the cathedral to confront him. There, the story is suspended, when Dickens dies.

"So, there you have it – a concise, in-depth report on the half-finished *Mystery of Edwin Drood*."

Freud's pithy summation confirmed that: (a) he completely understood the story and all its nuances; and (b) he knew Dickens as well as he knew himself.

As we enjoyed the next course of the imperial dinner planned by C. S. Lewis, I rested assured that the singular Austrian would slice through the tangled web weaved by Charles Dickens at Gad's Hill Place.

III

Professor Chambers provided relevant background information.

"Dickens's health deteriorated precipitously in 1869. He discontinued his reading tours and began to formulate a strategy for a new novel. He had been gathering material for a couple of years. By mid-summer 1869, Dickens decided that the story would involve (a) the engagement of a young man to a young woman, (b) their eventual breakup, and (c) much, much more. There would be twists, turns, and surprises. He chose the title sometime in September 1869. Composition began in October. By December, Dickens was proceeding nicely, but his health declined further. Notwithstanding his diminished strength, he gave a dozen readings from 11 January to 15 March 1870. Progress on *Drood* had slowed to a crawl. On 8 June, he concentrated on installment No. 6. There were to be twelve. No. 6 included the last lines that Charles Dickens would ever write – the chilling exchange between Dick

Datchery and Princess Puffer outside the cathedral after she shook her fist at the unaware Jack Jasper:

> The service comes to an end, and the servitors disperse to breakfast. Mr. Datchery accosts his last new acquaintance outside, when the choir (as much in a hurry to get their bedgowns off, as they were but now to get them on) have scuffed away.
>
> 'Well, mistress. Good morning. You have seen him?'
>
> '*I've* seen him, deary; *I've* seen him!'
>
> 'And you know him?'
>
> 'Know him! Better than all the Reverend Parsons put together know him.'

"That evening, shortly after he wrote the above words, Dickens had a massive stroke. He never regained consciousness and died on the following day. He was 58.

"The persistent question since Dickens's funeral has been: What happened to Edwin Drood?

"His eldest son insisted that Drood died. John Forster, his closest friend and associate, alleged that Dickens had told him about his 'very curious and new idea for the murder of a young man by his uncle and the recovery of a ring from the lime pit into which the body had been buried'. The ring would point to the uncle, who eventually would confess that he strangled his nephew with his scarf and threw him into the river."

Freud: "Haywood, thank you for the historical background. The historians, however, have fallen short. Obscure reports that have escaped the careless Dickens chroniclers tell us he collected material for two years before he began to write. The historians don't talk about what the dying author *found* during his research – the *facts*, i. e., the data points, which we will identify in the coming days.

"*The Mystery of Edwin Drood*, from beginning to end, was firmly planted in Dickens's fertile mind when he first sat down to write his final story. Only half of it made its way to paper. The other half will be revealed in what he came upon in his 1867-1868 research, before he chose the title. I imagine that he carefully laid clues that will lead us to what he had found during those years. We shall discover what unknighted 'Sir Charles' had found, and we will then know, with total confidence, the rest of the story.

"Pardon my drollery. I'm calling attention to the unfortunate fact that no formal distinction was ever conferred on our man."

Haywood: "A correspondent asked him why he never was dubbed 'Sir Charles'. A lighthearted joke had circulated about his being awarded a baronetcy or a seat on the Privy Council, the advisors to the queen. Well, baronet is a hereditary, nobility title – a status outside the reach of a commoner like Dickens. And, he had no desire to counsel the queen. The joke was mere banter.

"There were reports that he would be designated a nobleman of some sort. 'Our man' responded to all the buzz by saying: 'I am going to be nothing more than what I am; and that includes my being, as long as I live, your heartily obliged Charles Dickens.' He believed he had earned every significant distinction he could possibly have. The preeminent, Victorian man of letters never sought, nor was he ever offered, an honourary title."

Freud: "I must say, Haywood, his modesty impresses me.

"All that aside, we shall find clues that our high-minded hero planted along the row from Gad's Hill Place to Rochester."

CHAPTER 2

IMAGINATION

Inspector Gregory, to whom the case has been committed, is an extremely competent officer. Were he but gifted with imagination, he might rise to great heights of his profession …

Sherlock Holmes
"Silver Blaze"

<u>10 December 1925 (continued)</u>.

I

After dessert, our first snifter of brandy arrived, along with aromatic, Indian coffee. Freud expounded on Dickens.

"To understand *Drood*, we first must assay the author and his method. Dickens was much more than a consummate wordsmith. He was, as well, an instinctive psychologist who not only visualised the human mind but also saw that society impacts it. Dickens was Durkheim[10] pre-Durkheim, just as he was Freud before Freud. To comprehend this unrivaled writer, one must carefully read between his lines. There is much more to his method than elegant prose. He was

---

[10] Emile Durkheim (1858-1917) was a French sociologist and the progenitor of modern social science. He was the first behavioural scientist to make out the interactive relationship between the individual and society – something that Dickens, the skillful, self-taught observer of everything and everyone around him, had already started doing almost sixty years prior.

adept at so many tools of his trade: character, paradox, metaphor, simile, hyperbole, realism, imagery, mood, and *surprise*. Like Shakespeare, Dickens captured the essence of human nature. Better than any other writer of his time, he humanized good and evil in all their complexities.

"Although *Drood* is only half told, its themes are firmly set; and its characters are solidly in place. It is up to us to extend the plot to its *actual* disposition. Our findings will be solidly a posteriori – based on *facts* gathered through careful investigation and observation. Given what I just said about Dickens, I suspect that this story is *history*, not fiction."

"What do you mean by *that* audacious assertion?"

"Buck, let's leave it at that for now."

I shrugged. C. S. stared soberly at me, and the expressionless Professor Chambers nonchalantly sniffed his brandy and asked, as though he were on to something: "You're telling us that we should expect the unexpected, aren't you, Sig?"

Freud reacted with a mischievous grin. Nothing more.

II

He continued.

"It's time to analyse what we know by examining the personality profiles that Dickens has so smartly drawn. We shall first examine the five principal participants: John Jasper, Reverend Septimus

Crisparkle, Edwin Drood, Neville Landless, and Helena Landless. Princess Puffer and Mr. Tartar lie just outside the tight orbit of the major five. There is no need to examine them just yet.

A.

"Our initial focus is on John Jasper, the personification of evil – a split personality with a malignant, fragmented, criminal mind. I once described the criminal mind as 'a horrible wonder … which cannot be reconciled with the average intellect of any man'.

"Jasper leads two lives. Publicly, he's a reserved, austere, benign choirmaster. That brittle, priestly veneer conceals a dense inner depravity aggravated by the corrosive effects of opium, a fiendish palliative that gives him only ephemeral comfort before taking him back to the painful reality of his banal existence in Cloisterham and its confining cathedral. *We* see Cloisterham Cathedral as a sanctuary. *Jasper* likens it to a prison, just as he views the town itself – a secluded place where life has no meaning … a twilight zone where reality is unreal.

"Jasper is pervertedly attracted to Rosa Bud. Jealousy dominates his rancid soul. He plotted the murder: (a) during his opium-influenced dreams; (b) as he directed the cathedral choir; (c) as he roamed the cathedral crypt with Stony Durdles; and (d) when he entertained his unsuspecting nephew and Neville Landless, whom he had determined to incriminate as Drood's killer.

"A couple of years ago, I published an article titled 'The Ego and the Id',[11] a thesis on my theory about the structure of the personality. I believe the mind is tripartite. It comprises the id, the ego, and the superego – interactive, conjoined elements that assert themselves at different stages of one's life. The id arises at birth. It is the source of instinctive, primitive geste. It seeks immediate gratification. The id is the wellspring of blind passion, lust, sexual deviancy, and moral perversion generally.

"The ego is *reality* based. It issues from the id and tempers its blind, often evil devices and enables one to comply with society's rules or laws. Think of the id as a wild horse. Picture the ego as the horse's rider, who mounts the unrestrained animal, reins it in, and tames it. Absent its rider, the horse surrenders to feral impulses and does whatever it pleases.

"Even the 'tamed' horse is only partially broken. It has no *real* sense of right versus wrong. It remains an amoral creature in spite of its determined rider. The only 'animal' who can access the moral compass is homo sapiens, when the rider has found it and has it firmly in his grasp.[12] Then, the superego emerges from the ego, and the psyche begins to understand and hold dear the Ten Commandments. In regard to John Jasper, the rider is afraid of the horse; and he cannot bring himself to mount it. Jasper's id is in full control. At this point in the

---

[11] A seminal paper published by Sigmund Freud in 1923.

[12] Freud theorized that the superego surfaces when one reaches the age of five.

story, he is a morally bankrupt, shockingly evil person controlled by primal instinct. He cannot adhere to societal norms."

"Can Jasper reform?"

"I believe so, C. S. The answer lies in Rochester."

"Aah, yes. Rochester, Dickens's Cloisterham."

Freud: "Rochester is one of the earliest data points in a long, twisting series of *facts* that we shall dig up in the city so near and dear to Mr. Dickens. Our first stop will be Gad's Hill Place, where he died hours after writing the ghoulish scene where Princess Puffer shakes her fist at Jasper as he sings holy verses."

Reflective C. S. placed his right elbow on the table and rested his chin between the index finger and thumb of his raised hand.

"You have continually stressed the relevance of cold hard *facts* this evening. Moreover, you have suggested that the story is *history*, a true account of past event*s*. *Drood* is a novel, at least to the present point. Strictly speaking, a novel is *fiction*. This novel, thus far, doesn't even rise to the level of historical fiction. It is a far cry from *A Tale of Two Cities*."[13]

"I disagree, C. S. *Edwin Drood* is more than mere illusion with history as a strong backdrop. It is something far outside of historical fiction. Is it, for lack of a better term, *pure history*? Suffice to say, I am

____

[13] Note 74, infra. Dicken's pure historical novel about the French Revolution.

convinced that we can only answer that question by digging up *facts*, reality-based data points to be plotted and interpreted."

"Sig, I suspect you are closing in on *all* the answers. Is my suspicion sound?"

"Haywood, your suspicion is reasonable and, yes, sound. However, I have drawn no firm conclusions. We must always be mindful of Holmes, who, in *The Hound of the Baskervilles*, referred to 'the scientific use of the imagination'.

I return to Dickens's reference to Cloisterham:

> For sufficient reasons, which this
>
> narrative will itself unfold as it…
>
> advances, a fictitious name must
>
> be bestowed upon the old cathedral town.

I think I know what 'for sufficient reasons' means here. That dry phrase is, I believe, the ticket to the *Drood* resolution. The mystery will unfold, bit by bit, as we explore Gad's Hill Place and Rochester."

C. S.: "Why Gad's Hill Place?"

"Gad's Hill Place, near Rochester, was, as you know, Dickens's home, where he wrote what there is of *Drood*, and where he died. It very recently became Gad's Hill School. We must go there, before critical data points are erased. Some already might be gone. I imagine that Dickens left far-reaching clues for us at the site where his spirit left its earthly shell."

"Do you have in mind any other Rochester locations?"

"I do, C. S. The epicenter of *Drood* is Minor Canon Row, which Dickens renamed Minor Canon Corner. Other critical places are the weir and its surroundings. Our travels are not restricted to Gad's Hill and Rochester. We likely will go to London, perhaps to Limehouse, where opium dens abounded; and Gray's Inn,[14] called Staple's Inn by Dickens, where Grewgious had his chambers and gave refuge to the Landless twins. I have in mind yet another place in London, which I will identify later."

C. S.: "What do you hope to find at those places?"

"I expect to find *things, facts, data points*. That's all I care to say at this juncture."

"Something tells me we're in for an adventurous ride."

Indeed, we are, Mr. Lewis. Indeed, we are. [By 1925, C. S. had not pursued his DPhil, a degree that he would never attain.]

B.

"We need to refocus on the personality profiles.

"Crisparkle is Jasper's polar opposite: the incarnation of *good*. The horse has its rider, with his bridle in one hand and the moral compass in the other. There is *perfect balance* amongst the id, the ego, and the superego. Notice, I stressed balance. There is a caveat *vis-à-vis*

---

[14] Notes 1 and 9, *supra*.

the superego, which sometimes dissolutely transcends itself. That happens when the moral compass malfunctions, and the person affected becomes self-righteous and *faux*-moral. Morality slips into immorality. We see that phenomenon in Honeythunder, a proselytising buffoon.

"Dickens describes the young minor canon as 'fair and rosy and perpetually pitching himself, headfirst, into all the deep running water in the surrounding country … an early riser, cheerful, kind, contented'. The warmhearted cleric is the antithesis of the bleak, stealthy choirmaster, who, with no horseman, will never find the way to goodness and light.

"Jasper, Crisparkle, and Honeythunder confirm Dickens's prescient awareness of the id/ego/superego dynamic, which I constructed over fifty years after his death."

Freud paused and changed the subject, with a blunt, off-the-cuff admission.

"Everyone knows I'm *not* a Christian. Though I was born a Jew, I reject Judaism. I dismiss *all* religion. I regard God as an illusion and religion as a counterfeit defence against destructive impulse. I favor reason and science over irrational religious belief."

Well! – I thought. *So,* that's *how Freud sees belief in the Divine: mere pretence based* on *raw emotion. He's an atheist. Still, he can't mean what he just said! What does C. S. think about his frontal assault on religion?*[15]

Freud resumed.

"I *do,* however, recognize the cardinal role of *water* in Christianity. That ubiquitous, flowing marvel – the fountain of life that forms the oceans, seas, lakes, rivers, and streams and nourishes the Earth as rain – is the sine qua non for baptism, the symbol of trust in and reliance on Christ."

He again paused … and reflected. I saw doubt in his unblinking, squinting eyes and on his creasing forehead: *Is Freud the atheist pondering what he just said about godly water and baptism? Is he having second thoughts about religion?*

The introspective scientist emerged from his meditation and spoke as though he himself had just experienced the sacrament of baptism:

"Crisparkle nearly drowned as a schoolboy. He was rescued by Tartar. His near-death experience mimics baptism. He was refreshed and purified, just as he always had been after his regular morning swims in Cloisterham.

---

[15] C. S. Lewis, as of that time, was an atheist trending towards agnosticism. He was not so emphatic about his lack of belief as Freud was about his own.

In 1930, Lewis became a Christian, due partly to the influence of J. R. R. Tolkien (1892-1973), his friend and cohort at Oxford. Tolkien, a committed Catholic, was the famous author of *The Hobbit* (1937) and *The Lord of the Rings* (1954-1955).

[Freud consulted his notes.]

"The first four letters of 'Crisparkle' suggest Christ, Christianity's shining light. To shine is to *sparkle*, the last seven letters of his last name of *ten* letters. In *Genesis* 1, 'God said' appears *ten* times. He gave the *Ten* Commandments to man. The Passover lamb was selected on day *10* of the first month, as was Jesus, the Lamb that in *John* 12:28-29 and *Corinthians* 5:7 'takes away the sin of the world'. Just as God gave the Ten Commandments on a mountain, his Son, the new Moses, proclaimed His Golden Rule in the Sermon on the Mount,[16] which supplemented The Ten Commandments. Unquestionably, the Reverend Septimus Crisparkle is the story's Christ figure."

Oh, yes! – I thought, this time more deeply than before. *Freud, the* nonbeliever, *has researched the New Testament as well as the Old. He is lending credibility to Christ in a way that Pope Pius XI[17] does. Is a conversion in the wind?*

His steady hand drew a continuum on a page from his notepad.

o____o

Jasper   Drood   Neville   Helena   Crisparkle

---

[16] The collection of moral teachings by Jesus found in *Matthew*, chapters 5, 6, and 7.

[17] Pope Pius XI (1857-1939) was head of the Catholic Church from 1922 until his death. His aim was the unification of humanity under 'the royal scepter of Christ'.

"See where they fall along the line, which I shall call the 'morality line'. Jasper is at the far left, the sphere of immorality. Crisparkle lies at the far right, home to the internal sense of right and wrong. The others, at their earliest developmental stages, occupy various points between the extremes. We shall see how far left purification and *redemption* will reach."

I was struck by Freud's focus on redemption, Christianity's raison *d'etre*,[18] and gently interrupted him.

"Sig, do you think *redemption* is in the story's blood?"

He smiled ever so slightly.

"What do *you* think, Buck?"

"I suspect it is."

"Your suspicion is justified. I *imagine* that redemption is the story's nucleus. We'll have to see what Gad's Hill, Rochester, and London tell us."

"You're very much into imagination, Sig. Doesn't imagination fly in the face of reason?"

"Buck, imagination, or, as you Brits say, a hunch, is an essential fact-finding tool. By itself, it is impotent. We must go where it

---

[18] To Christians, redemption means that Jesus Christ, by sacrificing Himself on the Cross, set believers free from the yoke of sin or evil. To Jews, it is about God's freeing the Israelites from bondage, beginning with their seraphic journey from Egypt (Exodus 21:8). Redemption is a major theme throughout Dickens's body of work.

leads us – to *facts*, the data points that, if accurately plotted, bring us to solutions. Think of reason as your right hand, the symbol of strength, observation, and logic. Imagination is your left hand, which senses what you can't see, hear, smell, or touch. Discovery happens when your hands come together.

"Later, we shall draw *two* parallel continua with data points. The top line will include places and things. The other will contain people and ideas. We live in a non-Euclidian[19] world. Eventually, the two lines will converge at both ends. At those points of convergence lie what we're looking for.

C.

"And now, we shall talk about Jasper's nephew, Edwin Drood – inherent to the title, but not the story's predominant character, at least not at its midpoint. Notice his place on the morality continuum. At the beginning, Drood is rather far left. The frenetic horse is saddled and bridled, and its ambivalent rider is standing at its side. The horseman asks himself: 'Shall I risk severe injury by mounting this frenzied animal; or, shall I walk away, indifferent to the harm it might do to some innocent bystander?' That is the state of affairs as young, narcissistic Edwin so callously treats his vulnerable fiancée – simultaneously victimized by his megalomaniacal uncle, who terrorizes her and treats her as a sex toy. Edwin admires Rosa's beauty; and he is fond of her,

---

[19] In Euclidian geometry, parallel lines remain the same distance apart ad infinitum. In elliptic, non-Euclidian geometry, the lines curve toward each other and eventually intersect at both ends.

albeit in an immature way. He doesn't believe in her because he doesn't believe in himself. He's an unsteady, dissatisfied young man.

"Of course, his boorish, id-dominated actions are far less pathological than his uncle's. The rider is not so chary of mounting the horse as his Jasper counterpart is. And, with Drood, there is someone alongside the horse urging the rider to mount it. The intercessor is Grewgious, who condemns Edwin's selfish, disdainful conduct.

"That fateful meeting in Grewgious's chambers sparks a change in Edwin Drood. He has a transformative *tete-a-tete* with Rosa. Afterwards, and for the first time, he treats her reverently; and she reciprocates by shedding her juvenile attitude towards him. They part ways as true friends after agreeing to cancel their engagement. Frivolity has surrendered to sobriety. Edwin's ego has surfaced; the rider has mounted the horse and reined it in. His ego is firmly in the saddle, but will it ever hold the moral compass? Rochester will tell us.

D.

"To Drood's right lies Neville Landless, the dark, mysterious youth from the East brought with his sister to be educated in Cloisterham. Their mother is dead, and they were for a time reared and abused by their depraved stepfather. I reiterate the exchange between Neville and his soon-to-be teacher, when Neville tells him: 'It is well that he died when he did, or I might have killed him.' He adds: '[My sister] has come out of the disadvantages of our miserable life … as much better than I am – as that cathedral tower is higher than those chimneys.'

"In the Landless twins, Dickens portrays two traumatized youth – mercilessly whipped and cut off from society and, therefore, from its norms and rules of conduct.

"Again, the early dialogue between Crisparkle and Neville is telling. The minor canon's redemptive influence first comes to light during his initial exposure to the belligerent, angry young man from Ceylon. I'll repeat my earlier reference to their graphic exchange, where Neville candidly states to his new tutor: 'My sister and I came to quarrel with you and leave. But, we have come to like you. You generously received us and treated us like no one else.' With equal candor, his mentor responds: 'I will not repay your confidence with a sermon ... I will help, but you must also help yourself ... by seeking aid from Heaven.' Crisparkle, the redeemer, is teaching his pupil that redemption has its price – 'seeking aid from Heaven', i.e. from the Supreme Redeemer – Him, 'who gave Himself as a ransom for many'."[20]

My silent reaction: *Um-hum! There's a palpable thaw in Dr. Freud's once inexpugnable atheism.* I hastily and surreptitiously drew a 'religion line' on an index card, which I had subtly pulled from my jacket's breast pocket:

---

[20] Matthew 20:28 ESV.

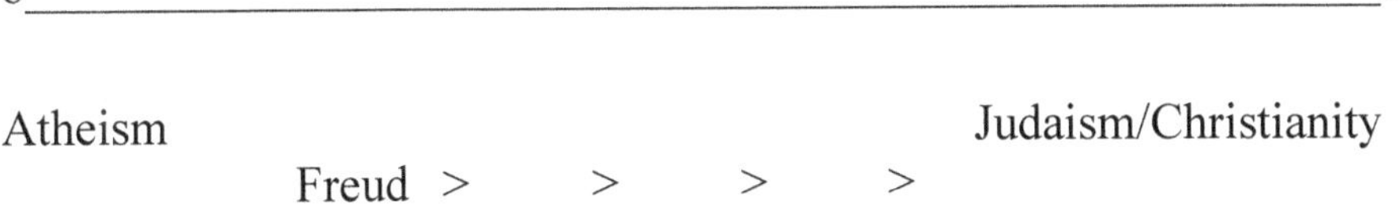

How much farther right will you advance, Dr. Freud?

He redirected us to his morality line.

"Gradually, there are rightward shifts by Drood, Neville, and Helena. At the story's transitional stage, only Jasper and Crisparkle remain at their original positions. The others, by the time Dickens died at Gad's Hill Place, are somewhat farther right. Here's how I see the transitions:

"Thanks to Grewgious, Edwin's ego has mounted the horse and reined him in. The moral compass hides rather far ahead, beneath a burning bush somewhere along the roadway to virtue. We know the burning bush from the *Book of Exodus*. The bush was afire, but the flames didn't consume it. The voice of God called to Moses from that bush and directed him to free and lead the Israelites from captivity in Egypt. After Moses completed that sacred task, he returned to the site of the burning bush, the holy mountain where God had given him the Ten Commandments – the guide to basic decency, the map to redemption.

C. S. squirmed in his seat. He was quite more dubious than I about our leader's budding embrace of religion.

"Sig, your continuing reference to religious texts and symbols and your declarations about Christ, baptism, and the Sermon on the Mount puzzle me. I find it strange that an atheist is so deferential to such things."

"There's a difference between 'deference' to something and 'belief' in it, C. S."

"Well, in your case, the 'difference' looks to be narrowing quite a lot."

Freud grinned, like someone caught with his hand in the biscuit barrel, and continued his morality-line narrative.

"Now, back to Neville, who is also moving rightward. Just as Grewgious has shown Edwin the path to righteousness, the shepherd of Rochester is pulling Neville ever closer to redemption."

I asked, "What about Helena?"

"Yes, Helena! At Dickens's death, she's as close to Crisparkle as anyone can be without touching him. Unlike her brother, she never yielded to her id. Her ego mounted its horse very early on. By adolescence, her superego knocked incessantly at her psyche's door. Her ego is steady in the saddle. Its firm, left hand has the bridle in its grasp, as its steady right hand reaches for the elusive moral compass, which is lying in plain view beneath the burning bush.

E.

"It is time to don our deerstalkers[21] and head to Gad's Hill Place, where we will find indispensable clues leading us to Rochester and then to London. *Edwin Drood* was conceived at Dickens's desk, facing the wide windows of his study. He composed most, if not all, of the story in his little hideaway that he called the 'Swiss Chalet',[22] near the main house. He will lead us to the *real* ending from his perch in his study, in the house itself – where he spent most of his final moments. Something exciting awaits us there. What we find will bring us to Rochester and the shocking data points that will direct us to London."

"How do you know we'll find 'something exciting' at Gad's Hill?"

"I don't *know* it, Buck. I *imagine* it. Remember our friend Holmes. In every case, he collected and plotted numerous data points, precisely examined them, and cracked mysteries that baffled all the other investigators. He possessed something that very few detectives had: *imagination.* Imagination and intuition, its first cousin, combined with logic and science, enable us to *see past the seeable.* Much more awaits us. What we shall come to see will startle us and everyone who hears about the fruits of our labour – the answer to the mystery. Jasper, Drood, Neville and Helena Landless, and Crisparkle take us to clues, which we shall plot along the parallel lines. Here's what I have in mind."

---

[21] A cap worn in rural areas, often for hunting. It is associated with Sherlock Holmes, although Conan Doyle never had him wear one. The cap is a product of the imaginations of illustrators and screenwriters, but it fits Holmes 'to a T'.

[22] Dickens purportedly wrote all of *The Mystery of Edwin Drood* in the chalet.

Freud pulled from his folder a white foolscap and drew on it his illustration of the non-Euclidian parallel lines to which he had referred earlier:

o____o
Gad's Hill School   Rochester

o____o
Drood   Helena   Crisparkle   Neville   Jasper

He put down his pencil and drew soft smoke from his cigar. As we enjoyed a few cups of steaming Indian coffee, the one who would guide us to the 'answer' told us what to pack for our travels.

"We'll be in Rochester and London for a fortnight. [By then, our leader knew we would wind up in London.] Pack as I suggested. Let's meet here tomorrow at 17:00, have an early dinner, and catch the 19:00 train to Rochester."

CHAPTER 3

THE CIPHER

Codes are a puzzle. A game, just like

any other game.

Alan Turing[23]

I

<u>11 December 1925</u>.

The train took us to Rochester Station, near our lodging – a two-bedroom flat on the top floor of a brown brick, four-level Georgian building on Rochester High Street, a few blocks from Rochester Cathedral and not far from Gad's Hill Place. The flat's spacious parlour was the ideal place to discuss whatever we might happen upon during our sojourn.

The parlour had been stocked with brandy, whiskey, and wine – prearranged by Freud, I presumed. He poured four snifters of Claude Chatelier cognac. Glasses in hand, we sat in comfortable leather chairs situated around a square coffee stand. We relaxed for two hours – talking mostly about Dickens and what he might have in store for us.

The late hour tapped our shoulders.

Freud asked: "What shall be the roommate arrangement?"

---

[23] Alan Turing (1912-1954) was an English mathematician, computer scientist, and cryptologist who developed methods that broke the German codes during World War II.

43

I offered a suggestion.

"Sig, since you already know Haywood fairly well, I think either C. S. or I should room with you. It's your choice."

He took from his pocket a musty shilling.

"George V, I bunk with C. S."

He tossed the dull disk about a metre above his right shoulder. It tumbled into his open right hand. He transferred the coin to the back of his waiting left hand. We saluted King George V. So, C. S. would fall asleep for the next fortnight in the company of Sigmund Freud, and I would retire with my old professor, Haywood Townes Chambers Jr.

II

<u>12 December 1925</u>.

Just a year earlier, Gad's Hill Place became Gad's Hill School. The rusty brick, Georgian country house was plain, yet dignified. We approached the front door, shielded from the elements by a narrow, protruding portico supported by two unadorned Greek columns. The door opened into a wide hallway extending to the back of the building. To our left, six metres or so past the entrance, a plaque mounted on a rich, dark-stained door said: "The Headmaster".

[Freud had chosen wisely to visit on Saturday, when the school would be free of students.]

He knocked, gently enough, and slowly opened the broad door. Seated with his back to us, at a wide desk facing the tall windows at the far side of the expansive room, was a bald, pudgy fellow dressed in dark flannel trousers and a greyish green, herringbone-stich, wool jacket. He turned in his low-back swivel chair, stood up, and extended his hand.

"Dr. Freud, I was pleasantly surprised to receive your call yesterday. I'm delighted to meet you. I attended your seminar in Manchester last year. Your views on the human mind are fascinating."

"Thank you, Mr. Lloyd. Allow me to introduce my companions from the University of Oxford.

"Professor Chambers, Dr. Bucktrout, and Mr. Lewis: meet Nigel Lloyd, headmaster of Gad's Hill School. He has so graciously agreed to show us around this room, the laboratory of the unequaled Mr. Dickens."

Thereupon, we greeted our host, offered our first names, and told him about our positions at Oxford.

Freud continued.

"Mr. Lloyd …"

"Please, call me Nigel."

"Thank you. Nigel, yesterday's phone call was rushed. I apologise."

"Don't apologise. The phone service is, to say the least, lacking. Neither of us could talk over that God-awful static."

"So, Nigel, may I explain in detail why we are here?"

"Please do, Sir."

Freud placed his left hand on the headmaster's rounded shoulder.

"*I'm* Sig."

The puffy, rosy-cheeked gent, who reminded me of a Baroque-era Christian cherub, nodded and directed us to a long conference table, where a pot of hot tea and a silver tray of quartered watercress sandwiches awaited us. As we sat down, a thin, attractive, young woman, who just had entered, poured our tea.

We sat down, and Freud began the discussion.

"I assume that *The Mystery of Edwin Drood* originated in this room."

"It did, Sig. Dickens developed the ideas for his final story at that desk."

He pointed to the fixture at which he had been sitting – a rather large, sturdy writing desk with a raised, angled top.

"This room was Dickens's study. The desk is where it always has been. Shortly, it will be sent to the new Dickens Museum in London.

[Lloyd stood and moved his pointing hand around the sides of the room.]

"Those bare, dusty book shelves, except for their missing books, are likewise as they were when he lived here."

Haywood: "I was on the property twice about a decade ago. On neither call could I gain admittance to this building, which was in the Dickens family's hands and not open to visitors. I'm delighted to be here today."

Freud: "Nigel, may we pause for a few moments?"

From his seat, he surveyed the tall, empty shelves, lining three walls. Then, for the next half hour, he explained to our excited host why we had come to Gad's Hill School on our way to Rochester and perhaps on to London.

Lloyd was spellbound.

"My, oh my! Your approach to solving *Drood* is so out of the ordinary! I can't wait to learn the outcome that has escaped everyone for fifty-five years!"

Freud: "Nigel, when were the books removed from the shelves?"

"A few weeks ago. They're in storage. The family asked us to send them to the Dickens Museum."

Haywood: "Oh, yes. The museum opened last year in 48 Doughty Street, London, where Dickens lived and worked from 1837 to 1839, when he published *The Pickwick Papers*, *Oliver Twist*, and *Nicholas Nickleby*, respectively. It is there that his international fame was born."

Freud added: "And, it is *here* that he left his final gift, an ingenious *oeurve d'art* that will end in a way no one has come close to envisioning."

Lloyd: "He left the unfinished manuscript on the desk after he just had carried it from the chalet, through that tunnel across the street.

[He pointed outdoors to the brick-lined tunnel that ran across Gravesend Road from the house's front lawn to the modest Swiss-style cabin, where Dickens wrote his final words.]

"The chalet is completely empty. It is scheduled to be moved to vacant ground near Rochester Cathedral."

Haywood: "Aah! The chalet, where Dickens wrote *A Tale of Two Cities, Great Expectations, Our Mutual Friend,* and, of course, *The Mystery of Edwin Drood.*"

"Nigel, do you have a ladder – the tall, rolling kind?"

"Dickens's library ladder is in the closet across the hall, Dr. Freud. I'll be right back."

A minute later, the solicitous school master returned with a narrow aisle-ladder on wheels.

Freud first conned those shelves he could see from floor level. He saw nothing but thick layers of dust. Then, he rolled the ladder to the far-left side of the wide bookshelf to the immediate right of the desk and climbed to the top step to examine the uppermost shelves as I moved him along the room's perimeter. We paused intermittently as the observant fellow on the rolling steps scanned every shelf along every wall – left to right ... at each eye level ... all the way to the end, at the opposite side of the study. He got down from the middle rung to the floor.

"Buck, let's return to where we started.

I moved the ladder to the point whence we had begun, and the man on a mission climbed to its very top – to the place that must have aroused his interest.

"Nigel, do you have a letter opener – the thin, blade kind?"

The helpful rector removed from the desk's middle drawer a thin, pointed, sharp letter opener; climbed a few rungs up towards Freud; and passed it, handle first, to his steady hand.

With a surgeon's touch, the man at the top, knowing he had found something revelatory, painstakingly separated from the extreme left side of the very top shelf something that had attached to it and hid impishly under dust and time. He slowly stepped down, holding a crusted card, yellowed by age and smothered by books. It was twice the size of an index card. Freud laid the delicate pasteboard on the table. Dense dust covered both sides. With his handkerchief, he softly swept away the crud. One side was blank. The other revealed a cryptic inscription, printed in faint-black, almost grey, ink:

DROOD … NACON … TICTA … NEAD

C. J. H. D

"Hmmm. Mr. Dickens has left us a vital clue."

"Like the Cloisterham/Rochester clue, Sig?"

"This card is more illuminating than Dickens's reference to fictitious Cloisterham, Buck."

I spoke under my breath to the wily fellow who must have been the second coming of Sherlock Holmes: *There you go, again. You keep your thoughts secret, until you feel the time for revelation is ripe. When that time comes, we'll* all *know why Dickens withheld the name Rochester.*

Freud scrutinised the card.

"Now, let's see if we can decipher what might be the roadmap to the true outcome of Dickens's last and probably greatest project.

"The initials on the second line are not code. C. J. H. D. stands for Charles John Huffam Dickens. That was easy. DROOD is likewise simple. NACON. Who wants to unscramble it?"

Straightaway, Haywood shouted: "CANON!"

"Yes, Haywood. Now, what about TICTA?"

Haywood did not hesitate.

"ATTIC."

"NEAD?"

Haywood was on a roll.

"DEAN."

"Bravo, Haywood! Dean – the head dominie at Rochester Cathedral. Dickens is playing a friendly, inspired game with us. He's leading us by our noses to the dean's residence, and its attic, at Minor Canon Row, or, as he calls it, Minor Canon Corner."

Our host was dumbfounded.

"Dr. Freud! I cannot believe what I just have witnessed! You all are on the cusp of a fantastic discovery, something that will shock the world!"

Lloyd paused.

"Am I being hyperbolic, Sig?"

Freud pursed his lips and glanced at the ceiling.

"No, Nigel. You're not being hyperbolic. You're on the money."

Freud's artful use of the clever idiom impressed C. S.

"'On the money'? Only the British and the Americans use that little phrase."

Freud beamed.

"I was introduced to 'on the money' at a conference I attended at Clark University in Worcester, Massachusetts in 1909 – to give a series of lectures about the interpretation of dreams.

"Nigel, the Manchester programme that you attended was much like the one at Clark. Psychoanalysis enables one to interpret sleep-induced illusions, which, as I said back then, 'reveal themselves as physical structures', usually sexual symbols.

He turned to C. S., Haywood, and me.

"Remember what I said on Thursday evening about the unconscious Jasper's opium-den vision in the opening scene: 'The spike rising from the cathedral tower is a metaphor for violence and eroticism.' I had also referred to its symbolic meaning at Clark.

"William James,[24] who had come to the conference from Harvard, invited me to dinner after my final talk. He declared: 'Dr. Freud, I think your dreams theory is on the money.' I asked him what he meant. He grinned and amusingly reacted: 'You've never heard that expression?' Blushing, I sheepishly replied: 'No, Professor James. I assume you're saying you wholeheartedly agree with my thoughts on dreams.' He reacted in his distinctively academic way: 'Yes, I am! 'On the money' means 'exactly right' or 'precisely accurate'. Your theory is generally philosophical, but threads of science course through it. I'm confident that, someday, scientists will confirm it empirically.'"

"The cathedral spike represents a phallus, correct?"

---

[24] William James (1842-1910), an American philosopher and psychologist, was the first academician to offer a psychology course in America.

"It does, C. S. We already have identified data relating to it: the personal interaction between Jasper and Rosa, where Jasper reveals his lust for her. We'll bring to light more data, tangible evidence, to bolster my opinion."

As we prepared to leave, Freud asked Lloyd: "Nigel, can you think of anything else, here or outside of this room, that Dickens might have left us?"

Lloyd folded his short, chubby arms against his diaphragm. A few seconds passed.

"There *is* something I found jammed in his desk."

He went to the desk; opened the wide, middle drawer; pulled out two restored newspaper pages; unfolded them; and placed them on the table.

"These pages had been rumpled and torn. I taped and pressed them. They are news reports of a terrible 1855 rail crash near London and a frightening 1865 derailment at Staplehurst, near Rochester."

Freud read to us the lines below, stopped, and kept the rest of the article to himself.

DAILY NEWS

London, 12 September 1855

Five passengers died, and seventy-five were critically injured, yesterday – when an outbound train from Dover derailed ten kilometres outside London. A railway spokesman said it is a miracle only five persons were killed outright ...

He proceeded to the next clipping, a brief account that he read aloud in its entirety:

DAILY NEWS

London, 10 June 1865

The Southeastern Railway Folkstone to London derailed yesterday where a section of track had been removed for engineering purposes. Ten were killed, and forty were injured. On the train was Charles Dickens, who tended the victims, some of whom died.

"I assume you all are familiar with the 1865 incident ... I know that Haywood is."

He turned back to the 1855 story and jotted something down. I asked him what.

"*Names*, Buck. They might be clues."

"Of course. I should realize by now there is method to your madness."

"'Method to my madness'. You mean I always act in a calculating way. The detective/scientist should always proceed according to a plan based on evidence and method, not blind supposition."

Haywood furnished some background information.

"*The Daily News* was founded in 1846 by Dickens, who was its editor for the first seventeen issues. He relinquished his duties to his friend, John Forster, but he remained an avid *Daily News* reader until he died."

Freud: "Haywood, the Folkstone accident no doubt resurrected Dickens's repressed memories of 1855. The newspaper pieces are additional data points.

"Nigel, please preserve these pages."

"You four are on a knightly mission. You may *have* them, and you may have this card. I know you will use them wisely."

Freud was touched. He extended his hand and thanked the munificent Mr. Lloyd.

"Nigel, is there anything I may do for *you*?"

"Yes, kind sir. May I have the list of names you copied from the newspaper article?"

"Why do you want this untidy list?"

"Because it's *your* handwriting. It's the perfect memento of this auspicious meeting. Besides, you don't need it. You have its source."

"True, my friend. The list is yours ...

"Nigel, we might have to examine the books that are in storage. If this card and these clippings lead us to where I think they will, the books will be irrelevant. Should we need to see them, will you arrange a time for us to do so?"

"Of course! I'll not ship them to London until you say it's okay."

As we left Gad's Hill School, I asked: "What's next?"

Freud: "We have lunch. Then, we retire to the flat, enjoy some wine, talk about Monday, rest, and then experience what there is of Rochester's night life."

"What's on for tomorrow?"

"Tomorrow is Sunday, your day of worship, Haywood. You, like Buck, are a devoted Christian."

"I am, Sig. Thanks for being so selfless."

"Well," said C. S., "*I* so far have avoided religion. Sig, what shall you and I do tomorrow?"

"I yield to you."

"I would love to talk about your time at Clark University."

"That's a fine idea! I can't think of a better place than the old cathedral town to relive my Clark experience."

III

13 December 1925.

We slept until 09:30 and had Sunday brunch at The Butcher's Block. C. S. and Freud transferred to the bar to begin their discussions, over Champagne, about Freud's 1909 lectures. Haywood and I walked leisurely to Rochester Cathedral for the 11:00 Eucharist.

CHAPTER 4

THE SEARCH INTENSIFIES

Take nothing on its looks. Take everything on evidence. There's no better rule.

Mr. Jaggers
Great Expectations

<u>14 December 1925</u>.

I

We sat down to a simple breakfast in our parlour. Freud showed us a sheet of bond paper containing various inscriptions.

"I entered some initial data points. On the top line are places and documents. The line below lists individuals and matters associated with them. When *all* the data points are plotted, the parallel lines will collide at both poles. Then, we will have reached our goal.

o____o
Gad's Hill School   **Rochester**

***Code

***Newspaper articles

o____o
Drood   **Jasper**
*Mystery   *Cloisterham
*Druid
*Drood's words to   *Encounter at Nuns'
Jasper about his father   House (Jasper and Rosa)

56

"On this seminal diagram, I placed three stars beside the top-line clues and only one next to those on the bottom line. I did so because the top-line items carry three times the corroborative weight of those below them. Were it not for those initial top-line leads, we would be on a rudderless ship, sailing to Nowhere.

A.

"The first data point on the lower line is the title's second word: 'Mystery'. I think Dickens intends 'mystery' to mean 'something that remains unsettled until the very end'. We shall solve the disappearance itself conclusively. Rochester will bare the other secret – something no one ever considered. Unlike those before us, we shall ground our findings on empirical evidence.

B.

"The second clue is the hidden meaning of the title's final word: 'Drood', the eponymous character at the heart of the mystery. 'Drood', I believe, is an alteration of 'Druid', an ancient Celtic priest or wizard, someone capable of performing magic.

C.

"The third tip-off: Cloisterham, meaning 'Cathedral town', is the fabricated name for a bona fide city, Rochester, the place that will yield the mother lode of data points.

D.

"The next clue is part of the extended conversation between Edwin and his uncle, which I didn't mention at the Randolph, when he says: 'My dead and gone father and Pussy's (Rosa's) dead and gone father must needs marry us by anticipation.'

"Dickens doesn't tell us outright how either father died. Instead, he leaves it to us to determine. The 1855 *Daily News* piece, included on the top line, will enlighten us. I'll leave it at that for now.

E.

"Next is the code – on the top line: DROOD ... NACON ... TICTA ... NEAD. As Haywood observed, the last three jumbles of that clever cryptograph translate as CANON ... ATTIC ... DEAN. Boz[25] wants us to visit the Dean of Rochester Cathedral, who probably lives at the onetime residence of Reverend Septimus Crisparkle. I'll bet ten pounds to a shilling that we'll find ourselves in the attic at the dean's house in Minor Canon Row.

[I beheld the man who had taken three enthusiastic Oxonians under his wings.]

F.

"The newspaper pieces about the train wrecks are likely related to another clue: 'Druid'. There are other critical data points in those news accounts. It's premature to mention them now."

"Sig, on what do you base conclusions concerning the train incidents?"

---

[25] *Sketches by Boz* (1833-1836) is amongst Dickens's earliest fiction – a series of pen-portraits and stories written under the nickname Boz. Freud knew Dickens had chosen the Boz pseudonym to identify the illustrations and stories as his own.

"Buck, I haven't *concluded* anything about intimations associated with the train mishaps. At this juncture, I *imagine* the connection."

I brought up something tangential: religion.

"Well, why hasn't imagination taken you to religion?"

Freud frowned. *Did I offend him?* I quickly recanted.

"Sig, I apologize. That question is … indecorous."

His frown became a smile, much as a hard bulb blossoms into a gentle flower.

"Buck, I'm not at all offended. I am a worldly creature. The spiritual realm is foreign to me. I see religion as a mirage. Imagination leads us to things in the *material* world. Data points constitute *empirical* evidence – something in *this* world that we can see, hear, touch, and feel. To say that imagination can bring one to religion is to say that imagination is faith. I have not made the leap to faith."

"Do you believe you ever will?"

Something struck Freud.

"I just said imagination is not faith. But, on second thought, don't strands of faith cut across imagination? Isn't faith imagination's sibling? I never thought of imagination and faith in that way … until just now."

Might our friend's distaste for religion be melting away? I remembered his 'spirit' remark at the Macdonald Randolph, when we spoke of Gad's Hill Place: "We must go there, before all-important data points are erased … I imagine that Dickens left something substantial for us at the site where his spirit left its earthly shell." I further asked myself: *If he believes in the* spirit, *he* must *be at least marginally religious; but does he believe there is a spirit within each of us?* We did not yet realise it, but Christmas Day at Westminster Abbey loomed large.

II

We followed Freud down to the lobby, where the building's lone phone sat on a credenza situated below an oil-on-canvas depiction of George V.[26]

"Operator, can you connect me to the residence of Dean Jeremy Roundtree? His address is in Minor Canon Row."

A long minute passed.

"Reverend Roundtree, I am Sigmund Freud. My colleagues and I are in town on a venture relating to *The Mystery of Edwin Drood.* May we by any chance visit you tomorrow morning?"

Freud listened for the better part of three minutes.

"Thank you, Reverend Roundtree. Thank you *very much.* Goodbye.

"Fellows, the reverend has hoped for and expected a call like this for a long time. He seemed happy … and relieved. He will see us at 10:00 tomorrow in #3 Minor Canon Row."

––––––––––––––––––––

[26] George V (1885-1936), the figure on the dull shilling that earlier settled the roommate pairings, was king of the UK and its possessions from 1910 until his death in 1936.

As we left for a walk around town, Freud asked: "By the way, Buck and Haywood, how was your visit to Rochester Cathedral?"

Haywood: "There is an eerie redolence about it – a malign spirit floating through its aisles and bays. Yet, I saw redemption peeking from behind its hallowed walls.

Freud rested his hand on Haywood's shoulder and looked him in the eye.

"Haywood, you sensed the presence of Princess Puffer... and John Jasper."

"*I* felt a calming aura – something reassuring and benevolent."

"Crisparkle's spirit touched *you*, Buck."

I returned to the subject of spiritualism.

"Methinks you may be crouching, like the Landless twins, Sig."

"Crouching?"

"One crouches before he leaps. Are you about to take the leap to the spiritual world ... and to *religion*?"

Resembling the cat that ate the canary, Freud grinned and said: "No comment, Dr. Bucktrout."

Rochester beckoned. We consumed the day roaming about its medieval streets.

CHAPTER 5

SECRETS

And above all, watch with glittering eyes the whole world around you because the greatest secrets are always [tucked away] in the most unlikely places. Those who don't believe in magic will never find [them].

Roald Dahl[27]

<u>15 December 1925</u>.

I

Freud at breakfast: "I anticipate a trove of evidence – palpable clues – in #3 Minor Canon Row."

Around a corner at Rochester Cathedral on a lonely, narrow, cobbled street sat a succession of seven contiguous townhouses. They were refined, trilevel, rusty-red brick Georgian structures bearing the numbers 1 through 7, painted in gold on sturdy front doors of various gleaming colours. Minor Canon Row was just as Dickens had described 'Minor Canon Corner': "[r]ed brick walls ... toned down in colour by time ... [with] latticed windows ..."

Freud knocked at the solid, deep emerald door marked with a bold, gold '3'. A lithesome lass, who appeared to be thirty at most, opened the door. She was tall and svelte. Her face was pleasant, and her

---

[27] Roald Dahl (1916-1990) was a British novelist and short-story writer.

nose was pleasingly symmetrical. She had a model's cheekbones; a firm but modest chin; clear, blue eyes; nicely coiffed blond hair; and an inviting smile.

"Good morning, Sirs. Dr. Freud, Professor Chambers, and Drs. Bucktrout and Lewis, I presume. I'm Margaret Roundtree. Welcome to Minor Canon Row. I'll take you to the study."

C. S. bowed and, in a graciously polite way, corrected our kind hostess.

"It's *Mr.* Lewis, Miss Roundtree. Unlike my ambitious colleague [motioning towards me], I have not earned my DPhil. I'm still grappling with the minutiae of my dissertation."

"I beg your pardon, Sir. I should have known better."

C. S. liked to poke fun at himself.

"No need to apologize, Margaret. Your assumption about by credentials was warranted. How were you to know that I'm an undisciplined, irresolute bloke?"

[Good-natured laughter all-round.]

We followed Margaret down the hall to a formidable room reminiscent of the headmaster's office at Gad's Hill Place. Books upon books covered every wall, save for the windowed one behind the imposing walnut desk of Rochester's dean, head of the Chapter of Canons at Rochester Cathedral. That middle-age gentleman, somewhere in his fifties, sat behind the attractive piece of furniture, burdened only by a leather-lined, green-felt mat. He was carefully making notations in the margin of the front page of a newspaper. Reverend Jeremy Roundtree was methodical, structured, precise, and no-nonsense.

He looked up, rose from his high-back, royal-blue leather chair, and gracefully walked around his desk to greet us. He was pleasingly tall and, like his daughter, gracefully lean. His high-bridged nose and steel-grey eyes indicated alertness and decisiveness. His confident, square chin told me he was a man of conviction. I thought: *How can this rock-firm gent show such a warm, gentle smile?*

He extended his hand, first to Freud, whom he plainly recognised, and then to me, Haywood, and C. S. His grip was solid and reassuring.

"Gentlemen, it's so good to see you. There is much to discuss."

"Thank you for agreeing to see us, Dean Roundtree. I'm Sigmund Freud. Allow me to introduce my associates."

After the introductions, our attentive host led us through a series of finely appointed rooms to the rear of the stately house. The day room was a tranquil space furnished with a long, brown leather sofa; its two matching chairs; and a marble-top coffee table. Margaret arrived with a raised-edge tray holding a thick, white porcelain coffee pot; six china cups and saucers; six Sterling silver teaspoons; a small china bowl filled with brown sugar cubes; and a china pitcher of frothy, hot milk. I was taken with the whiteness of it all. It was a courtly display delivered by an equally courtly, young woman, who, I thought, must closely resemble her mother.

Her father clearly was proud of her.

"Gentlemen, Margaret is on Christmas break from Cambridge."

"What are you studying at Cambridge, Margaret?"

"I'm pursuing my PhD in clinical psychology, Dr. Freud. I'll soon complete my required year of master's postgraduate study before actually starting the PhD phase."

"Well, how interesting!"

"By the way, Sir, I have studied your cogent theory about the id, the ego, and the superego. I trust it completely."

The compliment pleased Freud.

"Dean Roundtree, may we include Margaret in our discussions? ... Wait ... I shouldn't be so assuming. Margaret, would you like to join us, provided that your father consents?"

"Dad, are you okay with my participating in your meetings?"

"Of course, Margaret. Your dear mother, bless her soul, would approve, as well."

Freud kindly asked: "Dean Roundtree, how long have you been a widower?"

"My wife passed away a year ago. She was a victim of depression and took her life by overdosing on opium."

"Opium lies near the heart of our visit."

"I know, Dr. Freud. I know."

How does he know? – I decided to keep my question to myself ... for the time being. *This gentleman is about to reveal many secrets. They're all somewhere in this house. I can't wait to see the attic.*

We passed the next two hours talking about the subject at hand. Reverend Roundtree had dissected the story, as did his erudite daughter, whose *Drood* character-analyses paralleled Freud's.

C. S. was captivated by the stark similarity between the views of the Founder of Psychoanalysis and those of the immensely credible pre-doctoral student.

"Margaret, Dr. Freud and you have reached identical conclusions about the personalities of the primary characters. You did so independently. I'm impressed!"

II

The round-faced Victorian grandfather clock, oblivious to everything except its tick-tock rhythm and the hollow sound of its chimes, signaled Noon's arrival. Roundtree was prepared for that inevitable visitor.

"Follow me."

At the centre of the dining room's light, wood-paneled wall, to our left as we entered, was a deep, dark fireplace framed by a simple, wooden mantel, painted in white enamel. Hanging over it was Queen Victoria, on grainy canvas. The opposite wall was home to a high-grade oil portrait of Charles Dickens.

Haywood was drawn to the chapfallen, weathered face that once upon a time was gay and smooth. I, too, was stirred by the pitiable countenance. *So deep are the lines in his face!*

"Jeremy (we had agreed in the dayroom to dispense with formality), who did this awesome likeness of Dickens in his declining years?"

"Haywood, the artist will emerge, I promise. If you look closely at the bottom right of the portrait, you'll see the year he completed it: 1868."

"Why can't you tell us now who the artist is?"

Roundtree hesitated and looked at Freud, who calmly stated: "Because, Haywood, the data points must be identified in proper sequence."

I was a little irritated by the dual evasion of Haywood's appropriate question.

"Sig, Jeremy and you know something you're not revealing."

"Buck, please trust me as we continue our quest. Do you trust me? Do all of you trust me?"

His tone was pure and sincere.

"Yes. We trust you, Sig."

"Thank you, Buck. Thank you all."

Haywood remained fixated on Dickens, deftly portrayed by someone who spent countless hours recreating him just as he must have appeared in 1868: wrinkled, with a scraggly, greying beard and thinning hair; sad; and ill.

"That painting entrances you, Haywood."

"Yes, Buck. It does. Though I'm seeing it for the first time, it's familiar. Those sensitive brushstrokes are out of the ordinary. I don't remember when or where I saw that same adroit touch before."

I noticed Freud – staring at Haywood with frozen, piercing eyes. He was on the scent of something that would come to shock every devotee of Western literature.

We took our seats at the august Chippendale dining table. I surveyed the room, with its quarter-sawn oak floor and cheerful chandelier, which appeared to be 18th-century English. The table rested on a maroon Oriental rug with intricate floral patterns of powder blue, celadon green, and ivory. *Everything* – the table and the cushioned chairs around it, the flawless wood floor, the glistening chandelier, the velvety smooth white ceiling, and the soft-yellow walls – was most impressive. Yet, the striking feature in the dining room in #3 Minor Canon Row was the eye-catching, expertly crafted image of Charles John Huffam Dickens.

Margaret brought in an ample platter of sandwiches and wine. For an hour or so, we enjoyed lunch and touched on Dickens's life in Gad's Hill Place and Rochester.

III

Early afternoon: time to proceed.

Freud: "Jeremy, as you know, we are here to determine whether or not you can help us break the *Drood* code. I believe all the prior exercises are blunders based on caprice and guesswork. Dickens left a trail of clear, convincing evidence pulling us to the correct ending. We are here, Jeremy, to follow his clues."

He carefully lifted from his briefcase the card with the code words and the restored *Daily News* articles and showed them to the dean, who looked briefly at them before handing them back. He showed no emotion.

"Sig, my predecessors and I have waited since 1870, the year Dickens died, for someone to come here and unravel *Drood*."

Haywood: "Your predecessors, Jeremy?"

"Canon Joseph Cleary lived here from 1855 to 1875. He became Dean of Rochester in 1870. Cleary left a letter and its attachment; and a codicil, which he locked away."

In the study, behind Roundtree's desk, was a small, bronze safe. Its dark green door's keyhole was concealed by a thin, untarnished copper disk. He took a key from his purse and rotated the disk to expose the eager, mouth-like keyhole. I imagined the little vault to say, *Welcome, Reverend. I see you're about to show something to your visitors.* Roundtree unlocked the safe, opened it, and pulled out a thick, brown envelope.

He went to his desk. Margaret stood at his side as he carefully withdrew laminated sheets from their casing.[28] The documents were handwritten in blue ink on white bond paper, turned light amber by oxidation.[29] Holding the pages with steady hands, the oracle in #3 Minor Canon Row respectfully read a series of missives, by Canon Joseph Cleary and Charles Dickens, that paved the way to the attic.

---

[28] Lamination was invented in the early 1900s.

[29] Oxidation occurs when protracted exposure causes matter to gain oxygen, lose hydrogen, or lose electrons.

17 June 1870

To the future residents of #3 Minor Canon Row:

On 9 June 1870, Charles Dickens, arguably Western literature's keenest observer of human nature, left us for High Heaven's pastures.

I first met him on 11 October 1867, when he paid his initial visit to Minor Canon Row to inquire about old Rochester news accounts. Our first meeting lasted three hours. Mr. Dickens said he had begun research for his final effort, a story based on the lives of townspeople familiar to the Rochester community. I asked him, "Why will this be your last novel?" He said: "It will not be a novel, in the strict sense. At any rate, it will take over a year to write; and I believe I have, at most, a year and a half to live. Against the advice of my physician, I'm leaving for America on 9 November. I'll be there for a few months.

When I return home, I shall contact you to schedule some visits."

Dickens returned to Gad's Hill Place on 9 May 1868. We met seven times – in May, June, and July. During those memorable engagements, we discussed people, places, and events, all of which, over seven years earlier, had dominated the news in and around Rochester.

I made available to him various items that, through Divine Intervention, had found their way to #3 Minor Canon Row. They consisted of those things to which my visitor had intimated during his first time here –annals, memoranda, objects, clothing, and other effects. [I had organized everything in boxes and stored them in the attic's wardrobe.] I asked him if he would like to borrow them. He replied: "No, thank you. They must remain here, where God wants them. May I, however, take notes from them?" I assured him that he could.

After each meeting, the quiet, enterprising writer-researcher remained alone for hours, in the attic – examining and taking scrupulous minutes about all those abstruse objects, mysterious people (including me), and extraordinary events.

At the conclusion of his final research visit on 30 July 1868, Dickens appealed to me: "Dean Cleary, do you promise that everything you have shown me in the attic will remain there – safe, secure, and *secret* – until someone shows to you or whoever follows you as lord of this house, a card bearing code words printed in the upper case: 'DROOD … NACON … TICTA … NEAD?' He who has the imagination, foresight, and wherewithal to discover that card is the person picked by God to carry my story to its authentic conclusion."

I looked into his soul and saw pureness and light.

"My dear Mr. Dickens, I *promise* to place and keep under lock and key *everything* in the wardrobe. I shall reveal and entrust those items only to him who has the card; and I shall share our pact only with my successor, who will honour it, as will each person who resides here in the subsequent years."

He graciously thanked me. I saw him to the door, said goodbye, and watched him walk slowly into the shadow of Rochester Cathedral.

By noon on Sunday, 5 June 1870, I was at home from morning service. A deep, secure wooden box sat at the front door. I carried it into the study. Inside was a sealed envelope, addressed to me, atop a stack of papers about forty centimetres thick. I opened the envelope and withdrew Charles Dickens's letter, attached hereto.

Roundtree read the letter:

4 June 1870

My dear Reverend Cleary,

My remaining days are few.

In this box are the notes I took of everything in the wardrobe. I will not last long enough to finish *Edwin Drood*.

Please retain custody and control of these papers. When you learn of my death, arrange to see John Forster[30] at Gad's Hill. Tell him I handed over my recordings to you, and they are to be buried with me. Give him this letter as proof of your agency on my behalf.

I humbly ask you to accompany my casket, with the notes in your possession, to my burial service. Watch closely and see to it that the notes remain with me after you put them beside me, just before the casket is closed. Leave the funeral only after my interment.

Thank you, Reverend Cleary. You are a fine man.

Ever yours, Charles Dickens.

The dean returned to Cleary's letter:

Dickens died five days later. I learnt of his passing on the very next day. Immediately after I received the news, I took his letter to Gad's Hill Place and handed it to John Forster, who made sure I would place the notes with Dickens in his casket and remain with him until he

---

[30] John Forster (1812-1876) was an English biographer and literary critic, who was perhaps Dickens's closest friend and adviser.

was lowered into the ground on 14 June 1870 in Westminster Abbey.

Yours in Christ,

Rt Rev. Joseph Cleary

He then shared the codicil.

CODICIL

To My Letter of 17 June 1870

I implore succeeding clergymen who are plenipotentiary in this sainted residence to respect the wishes of Charles Dickens as I have respected them for the last seven years. Someday, someone will come to this house bearing the card with the code words. When that day comes, please give him unfettered access to everything locked away in the attic.

Rt Rev. Joseph Cleary

9 August 1875

We sat there, mystified and misty-eyed. Freud, the now tentative atheist, and C. S. Lewis, the wobbly agnostic, were visibly moved by Dickens's pitiable appeals to Cleary and his touching references to the Almighty. They had embraced wonder in all its glory.

"Well," said Roundtree, "it's time for a brandy. Margaret, do you mind serving?"

"Not if I may have one with you five!"

"You're in the group! Of course, you may!"

"How ironic! I don't have the right to vote,[31] but I may have a brandy!"

"You may have a brandy only in #3 Minor Canon Row, young lady!"

Everyone laughed as we retired to the dining room to unwind over snifters of Armenian cognac. A sudden question occurred to me: *Cleary ... Crisparkle?* I stole a look at Freud. He was not in the least startled. Nor were our host and hostess. I told myself: *They know what all of this is about. They know* exactly *what my Oxford mates and I will discover: Cleary and Crisparkle are one and the same.*

Roundtree: "Gentlemen, today was your introduction to Dickens in #3 Minor Canon Row. We shall be in the attic tomorrow and the next several days.

The attic: that metaphysical space described by someone years ago as "the ultimate guardian of secrets, the hiding place for all sorts of things disguised in darkness and dust ... family history ... the seductive part of any old house".

---

[31] By 1918, women in the United Kingdom who met prescribed property qualifications had the right to vote. The franchise was extended in 1928 to all women over the age of 21.

IV

Back at our quarters, Freud poured some port and took out the thick sheet of paper upon which he had drawn his first data points. Then, he amended and supplemented his prior non-Euclidian diagram:

o____o

Gad's Hill School   **Rochester**

   ***Code   **Minor Canon Corner**
   ***Newspaper Articles

      ***Dickens's portrait

      ***Cleary's letter and

         Codicil
     *Suicide/opium
    *****Attic

o____o

Drood   **Jasper**

*Mystery   *Cloisterham

*Druid   *Encounter at Nuns'

*Drood's words to   House (Jasper and Rosa)

Jasper about his father

"Think about all the entries, weighted according to their probative strengths. Apply your imaginations. We'll see if *your* imaginations take you where mine has taken *me*."

Freud, the hermetic Holmesian, was 'the safe plotter who plotted alone'. I told myself: *He will tell us everything there is to know about* Edwin Drood *in the attic in #3 Minor Canon Row.*

We had dinner out and returned to our rooms, where we talked about The Great War,[32] The Armistice of 1918, and the direful fuehrer of the Nazi Party. Like the resident of 221-B Baker Street, our newfound friend could set aside immediate, pressing matters and focus on other subjects. He expounded that evening on Hitler, whom he saw as an incipient menace, someone consumed by evil – an untamed horse that no rider would ever approach – a tyrant with an irreparably unbalanced psyche. *Hitler: shades of Jasper – I thought. There is method to Freud's discussion of the Nazi chieftain. He likens Jasper to the man behind the twisted ideology in* Mein Kampf.[33]

After we finished our port, Freud casually asked: "Do you all believe in magic?"

"You're referring to Dickens's likely derivation of 'Drood' from 'Druid'?"

He grinned: "Yes, Professor Chambers."

Midnight. Bedtime.

---

[32] World War I (1914-1918), in which C. S. Lewis served in the British infantry. Peace came with the Armistice.

[33] One of the seminal works of the 20th century, *Mein Kampf* is Hitler's autobiographical Nazi manifesto that called for Germany's world domination and Jewish genocide, among other atrocities. Hitler began writing it in 1924, whilst imprisoned for instigating the Beer Hall Putsch (1923), a failed *coup d'e'tat* by the rising Nazi Party. Volume 1 was published in 1925, and Volume 2 followed in 1926.

CHAPTER 6

THE WEIR, THE CAVE, THE ATTIC, AND THE WARDROBE

In solving a problem of this sort, the grand thing is to be able to reason backward … Most [detectives], if you describe a train of events to them, will tell you what the result would be … There are [a few], however, who, if you told them a result, would be able to evolve from their own inner consciousness what the steps were which led up to that result. This power is what I mean when I talk of reasoning backward, or analytically.

Sherlock Holmes

A Study in Scarlet

<u>16 December 1925</u>.

I

We arrived in our lobby at 08:30, wearing coats, rough khaki trousers, hiking boots, and wool hats. [Before we left Oxford, Freud warned us to pack those items. "We'll do some hiking," he explained.] He called Dean Roundtree.

79

"Jeremy, before we go into the attic, I think we should visit the weir. Can you meet us in an hour outside the cathedral?"

I asked, "Why the weir first?"

"Everything in the attic is there because of what happened at the weir, Buck. Crisparkle found Drood's watch and chain caught up on the dam and his shirt-pin trapped in the nearby muck. Those pieces of evidence indicate murder, attempted murder, accidental drowning, suicide, or intentional disappearance and concealment.

We're doing what Holmes did and what most investigators do today. We're reasoning backwards – looking at the outcome, the crime scene, first."

I protested: "We can't determine the story's finale at the weir itself. The weir won't tell us whether Drood died or survived."

"True, Buck, but *something else*, at or near there, will lead us to what we seek."

II

Roundtree, decked out for hiking, was standing soldier-erect at the front of Rochester Cathedral. A canvas satchel lay at his feet.

I stepped back to inspect him – to the degree that a commanding officer gives a going over to each troop in his assembled unit. *He knows or senses what Dr. Freud is up to. Hmmm. Does the good reverend know* exactly *what's in store for us?*

"So, we're going to the weir? I think I know what's up your sleeve, Dr. Freud."

"'Up my sleeve' … Buck, your English idiom must mean that our trip to the weir will give you a glimpse of what will come – things that I *know* but choose to keep to myself until the proper time arrives."

I bowed and said something so softly that no one else, except perhaps the sage from Vienna, could hear: *Sig, you're on the money.*

Our destination was a forty-five-minute walk from the cathedral. Cold mist dripped from a heavy, dark grey sky – a reminder of Freud's provident injunction to pack warm hiking gear.

We stood on a hill overlooking the weir – a passive wooden dam in a rushing tributary that fed the River Medway – where Crisparkle had found the watch and chain, clinging to splinters that refused to surrender them to the charging current. I took in the *mise en scene* and imagined the athletic minor canon – diving repeatedly into the frigid rapid, until the Sacred Hand pointed him to the watch and chain, and later to the stickpin lodged in the mud at the water's edge.

Freud's searching eyes focused, not on the weir, but on the hillside across the water. I asked him, "What is it about that hill that draws your attention?"

"Notice the bush at the base of the hill. It resembles a door. It's holly, believed by the Druids to be unearthly. Christians see it as a symbol of Christ. The red berries are the blood He shed on the Cross. The sharp, pointed leaves are the Crown of Thorns. In Austria, holly is called 'Cristdorn', German for 'Christ thorn'. [Veritably, the self-proclaimed atheist knew much about Christianity.]

"That bush is concealing more than the side of the hill. Let's cross over."

The only path across the hostile flow was along the top of the slippery dam, whose surface lay a few centimetres below the rolling water. It was less than a metre wide and about twenty metres long. Roundtree led the way. We walked deliberately, single file, and crossed the water in little time.

The thick, symmetrical bush was roughly 3 ½ metres high and 4 ½ metres wide. The space between it and the hill was about ½ metre. Freud, followed by Roundtree, squeezed behind the bush and disappeared. A German-accented voice, enhanced by echoes, resonated: "Come behind the bush. You'll see an opening!"

We entered a cave, sparsely illuminated by timid daylight that peeped through narrow openings in the rock ceiling, high above our heads. Additional light flowed from the hands of Freud and Roundtree, who used torches[34] to throw luminescent rays along the cave's dirt floor. Roundtree, who had packed them in the aforementioned canvas bag, instructed us to grab the remaining three. Momentarily, five lights scanned the dark ground, which must have covered upwards of forty square metres. The minor canon's light found what appeared to be a straw mattress with small patches of reddish-brown stain at one end. Shining his own light up close, Freud concentrated on the stain. We found nothing more and prepared to return to the other side.

I asked: "Jeremy, how did you know we would need torches?"

"You'll know before long, Buck. I believe Sig knew what was in this bag."

____

[34] Flashlights.

He looked at Freud, who turned to me and said: "I *deduced* what was in the bag, Buck."

I imagined what Freud somehow had already known: This was *not* Roundtree's first time at the cave.

III

The attic awaited us. We entered a pleasant, solitary, open area with a polished, wooden floor and a bright ceiling about 3 ½ metres high – the space that, from outside, appeared as #3 Minor Canon Row's top floor. Its naked windows, high above the narrow street, welcomed excited sunbeams. The room was neat, clean, and simply furnished with (a) a single bed made up with a sheet, pillow, and blanket; (b) a dazzling wooden table surrounded by six kindred chairs; and (c) an exceedingly tall, wide, deep wardrobe – standing at rapt attention upside the rear wall, well away from the windows. The dark-stained, solid-wood structure, supported by rugged ball-and-claw feet, was unlike any armoire I had ever seen. It almost touched the ceiling. Its wide, high door was equipped with an elfin, brass-framed keyhole. To this day, I *swear* that the breathing, pulsating thing on ball-and-claw feet said (I supposed to me alone) as I approached it to behold its majesty: *Behind my door lie things that will astound you and your two Oxford mates. Your esteemed friend from Austria, Reverend Roundtree, and Miss Roundtree know what I am about to reveal.*

I turned away and struggled to find composure. The others, talking amongst themselves about what we had seen in the cave, were unaware of what I just had experienced. I chose to say nothing.

The hospitable reverend had arranged the seating by placing name cards on the table. Margaret was at one end, opposite him. C. S. sat across from me. Haywood and Freud faced each other.

"Gentlemen, Holy Fate chose *you* to discover what you found at Gad's Hill School. As well, It led you to the cave. Divine Guidance then brought you to this room, where Charles Dickens worked so many hours, alone at this table, perusing everything that sits behind the door of that baronial wardrobe."

Freud was drained.

"It's 15:00. We have found much today. I ascertained long ago that psychoanalytic sessions should not be rushed. Probing the unconscious takes time and patience. So it is with solving *Drood*.

"Jeremy, may we conclude today's session and return tomorrow?"

"I agree with your strategy, Sig. We'll open the wardrobe tomorrow. Please come here for breakfast at 08:00."

We returned home and settled in the parlour.

IV

Freud drew on the top parallel line of his geometric model two new data points, 'Weir and cave' and 'The wardrobe':

o____o

Gad's Hill   **Rochester**

***Code   **Minor Canon Corner**

***Newspaper articles   **Dickens's portrait

                                         **Cleary's letter and
                                         Codicil
                                         *Suicide/opium
                                         *****Attic
                                         ****Weir and cave
                                         *****The wardrobe

He had reasoned backwards – to the place that laid the foundation for everything that would lead to a shocking post-crime admission.

CHAPTER 7

THE CRUCIBLE

If you shut up the truth and bury it under
the ground, it will but grow and gather to
itself such explosive power that the day
it bursts through, it will blow up
everything in its way.

Emile Zola[35]

I

<u>17 December 1925</u>.

Roundtree produced a long, golden-brass key and opened the armoire – wide and deep enough to accommodate everyone with considerable room to spare. We surveyed everything around us. On both side walls were shelves containing securely covered boxes. A clothes rack – holding a white, stiff-collared shirt; a blue, wide-lapel suit jacket and its matching trousers; a grey vest; and a pale red cravat – extended from side to side. On the wardrobe's hard plank floor sat a pair of brown, withered, high-top leather shoes stuffed with washed-out, knitted socks. A nondescript oil portrait of a plain young woman hung on the back wall. Freud took it all in. The lingering odour of old things seemed to invigorate him – mentally and physically.

---

[35] Emile Zola (1840-1902) was a French journalist, novelist, playwright, and political activist – a major player in the liberalisation of the French government during the last three decades of the nineteenth century.

86

"These items have been stored with utmost care. I see unblemished data points: hanging on the rack and on the wall, resting on the floor, and hiding in these boxes. We have entered the literary tomb containing Dickens's secrets. Here lies the whole truth behind *The Mystery of Edwin Drood*.

"Jeremy, let the games begin."

"The games began some time ago, Sig. They started in your imaginative mind and continued on to Gad's Hill School, this house, the weir and the cave, the painting of Dickens, this cloistered room, and this sacral structure on claw feet protecting things that are all too familiar. What do you want to see first?"

Freud pointed to the clothes and shoes. We took our assigned seats. Margaret removed the clothing items from their hangers and brought them to the table. Then, she re-entered the wardrobe, picked up the sock-stuffed shoes, and set them beside the clothes.

Freud, who would do all the talking for the next two hours, examined each article with the eyes of a jeweler, the nose of a bloodhound, and the hands of a raccoon.[36] He delivered his first remarks, entrancing statements that set the stage for the riveting *dual* conclusion to *The Mystery of Edwin Drood*:

"The faded clothes and the crinkled boots smell like brackish air – the air we breathed at the weir. The clothes are stiff and coarse due to saturation by hard, mineral-rich river water. Notice the stain across the back of the shirt collar. He who wore these clothes and found himself

---

[36] Raccoons have surgeon-sensitive hands and remarkable tactile ability.

in the river's clutch had received a blow to the back of his head before he hit the water. Everyone must have noticed the blood stain on the straw mattress in the cave. The boots are hard and unwearable due to the same hard-water exposure. They confirm my theory about the clothes.

"Alright, let's look at the girl."

Margaret rehung the clothes and replaced the footwear and socks at their place on the wardrobe's floor. She took down the rather small portrait and handed it to Freud. It was an overhasty painting on gossamer canvas of a youthful woman positioned against a barren, grey background. The framing was an amateurish construction of plain, haphazardly stained wood.

Freud held up the sham piece of art for everyone to see.

"This," he exclaimed, "is a travesty! The artist had little, if any, respect for his subject. His brushstrokes are aimless. His initials, H. S., are scribbled above the year, 1859."

Margaret returned the painting to its place in the wardrobe.

"Jeremy, shall we go to the boxes?"

The boxes on the shelf against the left wall were deep and larger than letter-size. On the right-side shelf were a compact, shallow box covered with grey felt; and its white, flat, letter-size companion – the thinnest of boxes.

"Which do you want to open first, Sig?"

"Let's open the small, deeper one on the right wall's shelf."

Margaret brought the grey-felt box. Freud gently pried off the top and removed three items: a gold watch and its chain, and a silver stick-pin.

I looked at C. S. and Haywood. C. S. had turned ashen. Haywood's eyes were glassy and still. I hyperventilated and focused next on Roundtree and his daughter, who simply folded their arms as they awaited Freud's next words. He turned over the watch and read the inscription: 'H. S.' Everyone, except Freud and our hosts, was shocked. *They're not surprised in the least! –* I thought.

"The owner of this watch, chain, and stick-pin was the sniffy artist responsible for the fake art that we just saw. And, he's undoubtedly he who wore the water-damaged clothes and shoes."

We broke for lunch in the dining room, where not a word was uttered. Haywood left his chair to revisit Dickens. Standing at his side, Freud looked past the brushstrokes and concentrated on Dickens *the man*. The person in the flesh and the figure on the wall seemed to be communicating telepathically.

After lunch, we slowly ascended the stairs – six 'priests' in a single line, climbing to the altar.

The brilliant table, which by this time had assumed a holy aura, was a piece of beautifully stained furniture made of solid, white oak. It was at the very centre of the attic – where Dickens had worked as he studied all the items from the wardrobe almost sixty years earlier.

I marveled at it: *This table is the crucible of truth, just as the Bethlehem Manger is the Way to Christianity.*

Roundtree continued the proceedings.

"Which box is next, Sig?"

"I think we should open the top box on the left-side shelf first."

Margaret placed it on the table. Freud opened it and pulled out a thick, red, leather-bound book. The pitch-black letters on the scarlet cover said: "Diary". The cover page: 'Diary of Neville Walmsley – 1 July 1860 - 30 June 1861'. Two red ribbons marked pages at the beginning and end of those that Dickens had chosen. Freud turned directly to the place marked by the first ribbon and read to us in the expressive tone of an actor:

12 November 1860

Past midnight. - - After what I have just now seen, I have a morbid dread upon me of some horrible consequences resulting to my dear boy, that I cannot reason with or in any way contend against. All my efforts are in vain. The demonical passion of this Motilal Patel, his strength in his fury, and his savage rage for the destruction of its object, appall me. So profound is the impression, that twice since I have gone into my dear boy's room to assure myself of his sleeping safely, and not lying dead in his blood.

13 November 1860

Woody up and away. Light-hearted and unsuspicious as ever. He laughed when I cautioned him and said he was as good a man as Motilal Patel any day. I told him that might be, but he was not as bad a man. He continued to make light of it, but I travelled with him as far as I could and left him most unwillingly. I am unable to shake off these dark intangible presentiments of evil – if feelings founded upon staring facts are to be so called.

The second and last ribbon took us to the unfinished journal's final posting:

31 January 1861

My dear boy is murdered. The discovery of the watch and shirt-pin convinces me that he was murdered that night, and that his jewelry was taken from him to prevent identification by its means. All the delusive hopes I had founded on his separation from his betrothed wife, I give to the winds. They perish before this fatal discovery. I now swear and record the oath on this page. That I nevermore will discuss this mystery with any human creature until I hold the clue to it in my hand. That I never will relax in my secrecy or in my search. That I will fasten the crime of murder of my dear dead boy upon the murderer. And, that I devote myself to his destruction. Motilal killed Haywood, and I will avenge my nephew's death.

Using a magnifying glass he had brought with him, Freud scanned the dire pledge that he just had read. *Yes! This phenomenal sleuth knew he would need a magnifying glass to examine documents. His imagination never sleeps!*

He put down the instrument, a clear, spotless, circular lens with a long, luminous handle – the kind of tool that sheds light on everything in its focus. He looked up, deep in thought, and said: "The magnifying glass reveals truth and bares secrets. It was made famous by none other than Sherlock Holmes.

"Through this revealing convex lens, I saw wild impulse. The paper is grey. It was lily white before time darkened it. The ink remains ferociously black. Jet ink on white paper suggests intense inner conflict.

The penmanship is manic. Notice the diary's cover and ribbons. They are scarlet, the colour of passion, seduction, and sin. The scarlet ribbons were placed by Dickens, who wanted to reinforce the tone of Walmsley's entries. The letters spelling 'Diary' on the cover are the darkest black. Neville Walmsley had been under evil's crushing influence for some time when he wrote those portentous words on 31 January 1861."

All three entries were *déjà vu* familiar. Along with Gad's Hill, the cave, clothes, shoes, jackleg artwork, watch, chain, and stickpin, they told us where we were headed.

Loud silence prevailed for the better part of a minute. Then, a shocking ejaculation: "Oh, my God!"

It was the uncharacteristic exclamation from the trembling mouth of Professor Haywood Chambers Jr., who expressed what C. S. and I were thinking.

"Haywood, are you alright?"

"Yes, Sig. I'm okay. I apologize for the outburst."

Freud was sympathetic.

"Well, I think we have done enough today. Jeremy, may we recess and return tomorrow morning?"

"Of course. I think a break at this juncture is advisable. Let's go downstairs for some well-deserved refreshment."

<u>18 December 1925</u>.

II

Margaret served breakfast at the Eucharistic table that had become the landing pad for all the remaining *Drood* pieces. Not much was said as we partook of what our hosts so graciously offered.

Freud had decided to change the order of things.

"The diary of Neville Walmsley leads me to believe we should next pull the thin box on the right-hand shelf."

It contained a single-page letter on white-turned-grey stationery. Freud again called on his magnifying glass.

"The script is neat and restrained. The placid, blue ink caresses the page. We see here someone in full control of his emotions."

Freud shared the letter:

23 November 1860

My dear Nev,

I am touched by your account of your interview with Mr. Cleary, whom I much respect and esteem. At once I openly say that I forgot myself on that occasion quite as much as Mr. Patel did, and that I wish that bygone to be a bygone, and all will be right again.

> Look here, dear old boy. Ask
> Mr. Patel to dinner on Christmas Eve (the
> better the day the better the deed), and let
> there be only we three, and let us shake
> hands all around there and then, and say
> no more about it.

My dear Nev,

> Ever your most affectionate,
> HAYWOOD STANLEY

> P.S. Love to Anne at the next
> music lesson.

"Here is an olive branch by Haywood Stanley to atone for his lapse of judgement during the argument he had with Motilal Patel.

"We have found most of what we set out to find. However, more questions remain. Though they're bending, the parallel lines remain on separate planes.

"It's time to open the last box on the left shelf."

Much deeper than its companion, it contained a tome-like, royal blue, leather-bound volume under a short, simple letter. The cover contained only the gilded inscription: "A*M*D*G."[37]

The letter was a provocative introduction to recorded events in the life of Reverend Joseph Cleary. Freud read it to his anxious audience:

---

[37] A*M*D*G stands for 'ad majorem Dei gloriam', the motto of the Society of Jesus. The Latin phrase, translated into English, is 'for the greater glory of God'.

23 June 1870

To the reader,

Those of the following pages tagged with blue ribbon by Charles Dickens are about matters relating to the disappearance of a young man in or near the River Medway on the early morning of Christmas Day 1860. He who gains possession of these memoranda will have happened upon them because Providence directed him to this evocative place, a venue for reflection about the missing youth. He who finds himself perusing the marked pages of this volume will be he who solves *The Mystery of Edwin Drood.*

Rt Rev. Joseph Cleary

Unlike a strict diary, the royal blue book did not contain continuous, daily summaries of its author's life experiences. Its entries were nonetheless chronological and seamless. Freud revealed the cover page, marked by a ribbon purposefully placed there and elsewhere by Dickens, just as he had done with markers of red in Walmsley's diary:

Remembrance of Things Past (1855-1870)

Joseph Cleary

All the script was royal blue, the colour suggestive of trust and loyalty – inscribed on fibrous, white pages, slightly darkened by 'the Man who carries the hour-glass'.

C. S. liked the title.

"*Remembrance of Things Past*. How interesting. That's the title of the Homeric Proust novel with which we are all familiar. Marcel Proust's[38] *piece de resistance* consists of five volumes. Additional, final installments, I believe, are scheduled for publication. Cleary's writings considerably predate Proust's. The original English translation is by C. K. Scott Moncrieff[39] from the French title *A la Recherche du Temps Perdu*, literally translated as *In Search of Lost Time*. Moncrieff's loose title translation is taken from the second line of Shakespeare's 'Sonnet 30':

> When to the sessions of sweet silent
>
> thought / I summon up remembrances
>
> of things past.

"Cleary couldn't have known about Moncrieff's translation, which took place almost six decades *after* he had given his own 'Remembrance' its title. Nor did Moncrieff know of Cleary's journal,

---

[38] Marcel Proust (1871-1922) was a French novelist, critic, and essayist known mostly for the classic novel, *In Search of Lost Time*, also titled *Remembrance of Things Past*, published in seven parts from 1913-1927.

[39] C. K. Scott Moncrieff (1889-1930) was a Scottish author and translator.

which has been sequestered for over fifty years. The dean *must* have known about 'Sonnet 30', however."

Freud picked up Cleary's scrupulous daybook. As with Walmsley's diary, he expressively read the Dickens-marked entries – more threads of evidence:

25 October 1860

A conversation with Neville Walmsley: Stanley is to visit him tomorrow and stay through the Christmas/New Year holidays. I tell Walmsley that his nephew's visit will help him more than a doctor would. He says he loves his nephew dearly.

7 November 1860

Mother and I are having post-breakfast tea. She holds up a letter, delivered yesterday. It's from Richard Myerscough. She reads it to me. Myerscough writes that he will bring his two wards, the twins named Motilal and Indira Patel, to Rochester to be educated. He confirms that I will tutor Motilal, and Indira will be schooled at Eastgate House, as per my recommendation. They will arrive on 12 November. I protest that the notice is rather short. Mother retorts: "It is what it is. We'll have to deal with the situation."

I point out that Walmsley's nephew is in town and would be a fine friend to our visitors. I suggest we invite the three of them to dinner, and include Walmsley; Anne; Myerscough; and Miss Meade, headmistress at Eastgate House.

12 November 1860

I meet Myerscough and his wards at the London omnibus station in Elephant & Castle. The Patel siblings are attractive and dark, with wild eyes. There is something parahuman about them. I invite Myerscough to the dinner.

At dinner, gluttonous Myerscough is loud and insufferable. Motilal and I hurry him away to the omnibus station, escort him to his seat, and quickly leave him.

On the way back to Minor Canon Row, Motilal says: "I know very little of that man … almost nothing." I find that strange.

He then talks about his and his sister's tragic, gloomy lives: They are from Ceylon,[40] where they lived with their stepfather. Their mother died when they were small children. Their stepfather/guardian terribly mistreated them. Myerscough became their custodian after their oppressive father died. I am taken aback when Motilal tells me he might have killed him had he not died. He defends himself: "He beat my sister, more than once or twice, and I never forgot it."

I decide that we should walk around some more, so that we could finish our discussion. I am particularly interested to hear more about Motilal's sister.

---

[40] Ceylon is an island in the Indian Ocean off the southeast coast of India. In 1972, it became the Democratic Socialist Republic of Sri Lanka. The king's/queen's English, spoken by the Patel twins, is common there amongst the more educated.

He tells me: "My sister and I came here to quarrel with you, and affront you, and break away again … we made up our minds not to like you … but we *do* like you … we see an unmistakable difference between you and anyone else we have ever known." He goes on: "My sister has overcome the disadvantages of our miserable life, as much better than I am … Nothing in our misery ever subdued her, though it often cowed me … She showed the daring of a man." I say to myself: *Motilal has taken his first step toward redemption. His sister is nine tenths of the way there.* I feel I must warn my student: "I will not repay your confidence with a sermon … If I am to do you any good, it can only be with your assistance; and you can only render that, efficiently, by seeking aid from Heaven." That earnest advice is my first lesson for Motilal.

Our last words before returning to #3 Minor Canon Row relate to Haywood Stanley, whom Motilal met, with Anne, shortly after his arrival. He asks about Haywood's relationship to Anne. I tell him they are engaged. He replies: "Oh! Now I understand his air of proprietorship!" My disturbing thought: *I see trouble round the corner between these two young men.*

We re-enter #3 Minor Canon Row. Anne, accompanied by Walmsley at the piano, is singing. She is afraid, threatened by Walmsley, it seems. The Patel twins descry her anxiety. Brother and sister, joined spirits, are communicating clairvoyantly about Anne's troubling discomfiture. Anne panics: "I can't bear this! I am frightened! Take me away!" Miss Patel places her on the sofa and comforts her. I notice Walmsley. He's the image of Satan.

Later that evening, Motilal, who earlier left Minor Canon Row with Stanley to escort Anne and Indira to Eastgate House, knocks at my door. I am at the piano, practising for the next church service. Motilal is vexed, disheveled, and squiffed. He says he was at Walmsley's house, where Stanley and he had a rabid altercation. Clearly impaired, my pupil says he drank little. The wine unaccountably "overcame [him] in the strangest, most sudden manner." He says his mind is "much confused" and recounts a series of troublesome events that led to a fight with Stanley. He clenches his hand – a foreboding gesture. I sternly order him to unclench his fist. He obeys, but shouts: "I would have cut him down if I could, and I tried to do it!"

After I calm him down, I bring him to his room and place my hand on his shoulder. He sobs himself to sleep. I see undiluted contrition on his sad face.

Someone knocks. I open the door. Walmsley, standing defiant whilst leaning leftward to favour his right side, tells me of the ugly fight between his nephew and Motilal. As I see the evil in Walmsley's dark, beady eyes, I conclude that he orchestrated the fight.

17 November 1860

Mother and I discuss the two young men who are seen as irreformable enemies. Their skirmish at Walmsley's house is the talk of the town. Mother thinks ill of my pupil. She believes the Walmsley-inspired gossip that he is prone to violence.

21 November 1860

After Vespers, I decide to lope down to the river. I run across the Patel twins. A conversation ensues. I urge Motilal to make amends for his offence against Stanley. They claim that Stanley is not free from fault.

I become angry when Motilal reveals his admiration for Anne and sees himself as her protector from Stanley's shoddy treatment. I declare to him: "It is monstrous that you should take it upon yourself to be the young lady's champion against her chosen husband." He responds: "Stanley is incapable of the feeling with which I am inspired towards the worthy young creature whom he treats like a doll … I love her, and I *hate* him!"

I exhort him to erase from his mind his infatuation with Anne and to make peace with Stanley. His attitude shifts, as Indira counsels him: "Follow your guide now, Motilal, and follow him to Heaven." I am moved when Indira says to me: "What is *my* influence, or *my* wisdom, compared to *yours*?" Then, she takes my hand and, in a gesture of reverence, gently kisses it.

On the way home, I pay a visit to Walmsley. He has been asleep. He jumps from the couch, frantically shouting: "What's the matter? Who did it?" I bring him to his senses and tell him I'm there to talk about ending the dissention between his nephew and Motilal. I ask him to persuade his nephew to send Motilal a good-faith offer proposing a cessation of hostility. Surprisingly, he agrees. Then, he shows me a bizarre diary account, dated 13 November 1860 – referring to young

Patel's "dark, intangible presentiments of evil ..." Before we part, however, Walmsley promises that his nephew will extend an outright apology for his inexcusable conduct towards Motilal. That placatory gesture, in light of the baleful words I just read, confirms that Walmsley's mind is rent by deep inner conflict.

27 November 1860

Lo and behold! Walmsley produces a letter dated 23 November 1860 – his nephew's unconditional apology and invitation to Motilal (through Walmsley) to join him at Walmsley's house for Christmas Eve dinner to effect their conciliation.

24 December 1860

Walmsley is in fine voice at Christmas Eve's Vespers. He has on his familiar black scarf as we leave the cathedral together. I compliment him on his steady, resonant voice. He says he will burn his latest diary at year's end and adds: "It shows my dark side, and it covers a period of my life I want to put behind me." Those are out-of-the-way words. I ask myself, *Will he burn it?* and conclude, *Probably not.*

Christmas Eve night is stormy. High wind blows down chimneys and damages rooftops. Is all that a portent of violence?

25 December 1860

The cathedral's roof is torn. Its tower is missing some stones. The tower clock has no hands.

Walmsley appears at an open window and accosts me: "Where is my nephew? He went down to the river last night with Mr. Patel to look at the storm and has not been back. Call Mr. Patel!" I respond: "He left for a fortnight's hike this morning, early."

A few hours later, Motilal returns – in the custody of those who must have gone to apprehend him and bring him back to Rochester. As Walmsley looks on, they hand him over to me. Walmsley accusatorily asks Motilal: "Where is my nephew?" His tone is acerbic. "*You* were the last person in his company, and he is not to be found." Young Patel is dumbstruck. He gathers his thoughts, and I methodically interrogate him about the events following dinner at Walmsley's. He appears totally honest as he spells out what transpired after dinner: Stanley and he left Walmsley's house and went together to the river, near a weir that tried in vain to hold back gushing water. They felt the storm's rage from a spot on a hill, where they stayed for a half hour and then walked to #3 Minor Canon Row. Stanley left from my front door and, Motilal assumed, returned home to Walmsley.

Walmsley persists: "What are those stains on his clothes and on his walking stick?" Motilal persuasively explains that the blood is from one of his captors, with whom he struggled as he defended himself in what he thought was an ambush by eight strangers. One of the captors admits that he and his cohorts failed to explain to young Patel the reason for their detaining him.

I refer the matter to Mayor Raferty post haste. At the preliminary hearing, I vigourously defend my pupil and pledge to maintain strict control of him. The mayor releases him to me. He orders that the river in the vicinity of the weir be dragged and its banks searched.

I closely watch Walmsley and the young fellow whom he has accused of doing in his nephew. Each is stoop-shouldered and forlorn – for different reasons. Young Patel is worried about his friend and former foe. Walmsley, however, is trying to cope with shame and guilt. I am compelled to think: *Walmsley murdered Stanley and is trying to frame Motilal for the crime.*

4 January 1861

I chance upon Walmsley and Mr. Blair, Anne's guardian, as they converse at Walmsley's house. In a complete change of heart (I doubt his sincerity), he says: "I begin to believe it possible that my nephew may have disappeared of his own accord, and may yet be alive and well." Walmsley is in denial. [Blair had informed him that Stanley and Anne, to whom he is perversely attracted, broke off their engagement.] He must think: *Damn it! I killed my nephew for nothing!* So, the only way to cope with his searing guilt is to pretend the murder didn't happen.

Protracted search at the river had yielded nothing. As I leave Walmsley's, Something (or Someone) orders me to take the short walk from the river to the weir, which itself was never closely examined. It is in a fierce stream that feeds the Medway – very near the site where the former combatants sat together as friends to watch the storm. When I arrive, it is too dark to see anything. Tomorrow is another day.

5 January 1861

It is sunny and cold. I focus on the weary wooden dam, hoping something will catch my eye. The Man Above (unmistakably the 'Someone' who directed me to this spot yesterday) tells me: "Turn away for a few seconds and refocus on the weir." Upon returning my eye to the spot it just left, I see an object, reflecting sunlight. I dive into the forbidding, icy water and swim against the current to the weir. There it is – a chain clasping a gold watch, with the initials 'H. S.' etched on its back. I take the watch and chain to the riverbank and return to the weir, where I dive and swim downward toward the water bottom. It is clear enough to see the bottom for six metres around. Nothing is there. I swim back to the surface and climb to the top of the bank. A thin, metal object is trapped in the mud. It's a stick-pin. *I have found all the personal effects of Haywood Stanley!* I dive into the water and swim to the bottom, again and again, until I can no longer withstand the biting cold. Stanley is nowhere to be found.

I head back to town with the watch, chain, and stick-pin; fetch young Patel; and go to the mayor's office. He summons Walmsley, who identifies the items. Motilal is arrested, taken into custody, and again becomes the object of hard-hearted, irresponsible rumours. But, behind the mayor's door, there is solid, circumstantial evidence of guilt: inter alia, Motilal's transcribed threats against Stanley; residues of blood on his clothes and walking stick (all retained by the mayor as evidence); Walmsley's recorded testimony about the explosive altercation at his house; and the watch, chain, and stick-pin, also preserved in the mayor's evidence room.

12 January 1861

The inquiry drags on. No new evidence has turned up. There have been no further allegations, other than wild innuendo. Stanley is presumed dead.

Although accidental drowning cannot be ruled out, Motilal Patel is charged by the prosecutor, who seeks to appease the clamouring public. He remains in my strict custody, under a quite sizable cash bond posted by an anonymous benefactor.

14 January 1861

The dean orders me to evict my still-besieged student. [I anticipated this lamentable development.] I am despondent, because I know the young man is innocent. He reminds me of the Bearer of the Cross.

Motilal is jailed. The bail is refunded to the 'maecenas', who is revealed as Mr. Blair, the discerning solicitor and the guardian of Anne Darwin. He furnished bond, he says, because he reveres the presumption of innocence as much as he loves fine literature and art, just as Maecenas, the Roman statesman and patron of the arts, did.

2 February 1861

Out of the blue, Walmsley shows me an entry in his diary, dated 31 January 1861: "My dear boy is murdered Motilal killed Haywood, and I will avenge my nephew's death." *How delusional!* He *is the murderer. Will he kill* himself *to avenge his nephew's death?*

5 July 1861

I visit pompous Myerscough, who takes me to task for believing in Motilal's innocence. He asks: "Then, who do you make out did the deed?" I react sternly: "I accuse no one." [In my heart, I know Walmsley is the evildoer; but I have no proof.] I chastise Myerscough for his incivility. What a hypocrite! What a churl! The only positive aspect of my visit: Myerscough transfers to my name the guardianship papers for Indira and Motilal Patel.

I proceed to London and Gray's Inn, where Motilal has taken up residence near Mr. Blair's chambers. [The prosecutor had dismissed the charges against the beleaguered defendant, and he was freed on 30 June to go wherever he wished. He chose Gray's Inn, where his sister soon will join him. [My chastened ward has followed my recommendation and is studying law under Mr. Blair at the Inn.]

It is a lovely visit. With welled eyes, the appreciative young man says to me: "You have shown me the light, Reverend Cleary. I thank God for sending me to you." I nod and smile whilst thinking, *Here is a young man well on his way to redemption.*

I hurry across the Walks[41] to Mr. Blair's chambers. He tells me Walmsley is in London. I'm afraid Walmsley is here to stalk Motilal and kill him.

---

[41] Notes 1, 9, and 14, supra. Gray's Inn Gardens, known as "The Walks," were laid out by Sir Francis Bacon in 1608. The Gardens, adjacent to the barristers' chambers in Gray's Inn, consist of tree-lined gravel paths that wind along attractive flower beds.

12 July 1861

I return to London to see Mr. Blair and assure that Anne, living nearby and shielded from Walmsley, is safe and sound. Anne arrives at Blair's chambers. She is concerned about the welfare of Motilal and Indira.

A gentleman enters the chambers. I earlier saw him at a distance, smoking under the trees in the Walks. Lo! He is Henry Davidson, my old schoolmate, who saved me from drowning. He says he has lived close to Motilal and Indira in Gray's Inn and will remain in London for a time.

Late of the navy, he came home to take possession of Highclere Castle, a grand estate left to him by his uncle. He wants to transition from military life by living in Spartan-like Gray's Inn before joining the ranks of the landed gentry.

I exclaim to Mr. Blair and Anne: "Imagine Davidson, when he was the smallest of juniors, diving for me; catching me, a burly senior, by the hair of the head; and striking out for the shore with me like a water-giant!" Just after those words leave my lips, I think: 'Damn! *I* was diving for Haywood Stanley in the same way on that cold morning at the weir!'

Anne sadly brings up her mother, whose life was stolen by merciless water. Water, on one hand the agent of salvation and, on the other, the sharp tool of tragedy.

III

Finally, Freud stopped reading. Like him, Roundtree and his daughter knew the ending. The composed dean announced lunch. We were emotionally drained and gladly followed him to to savour steak and kidney pudding, with some robust claret.

Lunch ended. I asked, "Will we spend more time in the attic?"

Freud thought not.

"Jeremy and Margaret, you know the end of the story. I think *I* do, as well. Buck, C. S., and Haywood know much more than they did before our time in this blest room. Still, they don't know whether Drood, that is, Stanley, survived; or, if he died, how? We should defer further reading until tomorrow.

"Before we recess, may we go back to the attic for just a minute? I noticed something at the bottom of the Cleary box."

117

We took our places at the table. Freud reached into the box and maneuvered his nimble hands along its perimeter, down to the bottom. He slowly pulled out a rather long, mauve, silk scarf.

"This scarf once was shiny and black. Time has dulled its lustre."

He passed it on to Margaret.

"We'll resume tomorrow; and, as the mayor said to Dick Datchery: 'We shall [continue to] build up proof stone by stone.'"

As we got up, I noticed for the first time a murky brass strip screwed onto the top of the inside back of Haywood's chair and took a close look. Inscribed in matte black letters was 'Charles Dickens'. I examined the others, none of which had any such adornment. Pointing to the little plaque, I asked Haywood, "Have you noticed what is on the back of your chair?"

"No, Buck ... not until just now. How did I miss *that*?"

Freud looked at Roundtree, then to my late mentor, and said: "There is a reason that the marker is there, Haywood, as everyone shall see in due course."

I chose not to ask our leader to explain. After all, he was 'the safe plotter who plotted alone' – the man who knew when the time for disclosure is up.

Before we broke, Haywood addressed Cleary's distant successor: "Jeremy, I took a few notes as Sig read Reverend Cleary's entries. His 12 November 1860 account refers to the piano at this residence. Might the piano in the side room to the foyer's right be the same one that is in 'Remembrance'?"

"Yes, Haywood. That fine 1831 Loud & Brothers upright plays perfectly to this day. I have it tuned twice a year. I am told that it was regularly serviced before I arrived here. It has stood in the side room at #3 since 1832."

Another stone ... another brick of truth.

CHAPTER 8
LE SUICIDE'

The term suicide is applied to all cases

of death resulting directly or indirectly

from a positive or negative act of the

victim himself, which he knows will

produce this result.[42]

Emile Durkheim

I

Dinner at The King's Arms on 18 December was hushed and reflective. Just before we prepared to leave for our rooms, Freud broke the silence.

"We are on a pilgrimage that will take us to the heart of *The Mystery of Edwin Drood.* I see awe in your eyes at the astounding revelations in the attic. I see, as well, your awe of Dickens. Aware that he soon would die, he left clues about Western literature's most baffling mystery. He left all those clues for *us* to find. From his grave beneath Westminster Abbey, he chose *us* to finish *Drood.*"

We walked silently to our temporary home in Rochester and went to bed. I did not sleep.

---

[42] Note 10, supra. Emile Durkheim's famous treatise, *Le Suicide'* (1897), is the first empirical study about the societal factors that might cause suicide. Durkheim is amongst the first social scientists to recognize the interactive relationship between the individual and society.

<u>19 December 1925</u>.

II

Cleary had left considerably more for us to read.

My knees slightly trembled as I took my seat at the glowing altar of wood, where truth shone as brightly as its glossy top. I braced myself for further stunners from the pen of Reverend Joseph Cleary.

Freud went to the next letter.

23 August 1861

I am in my study, reading *Little Dorrit*.[43] Knock … knock …knock.

"Mother, who is at the door?" ... Silence ... I get up to see what is going on. Pallid, and, for once, speechless, Mother is standing at the door with Haywood Stanley, Henry Davidson, Anne, Motilal, and Indira. I gaze at the poor lad who went missing on Christmas Day, eight months ago. He was frail, much unlike the lusty youth whom I last saw shortly before he disappeared.

---

[43] *Little Dorrit* (1857) is perhaps Dickens's harshest criticism of government bureaucracy. As well, the novel exposes the pronounced stratification of society and the harsh realities of prison life.

"Davidson, what, for Heaven's sake, is *this*?!"

We proceed to the dining room. I sit at the head of the table. Davidson is opposite me. To my right, in his direction, are, first, Indira and then Stanley. To my left, in the same direction, are Anne and Motilal. I survey the scene and wonder: *What led my unexpected guests to choose their individual places at the table? Does this arrangement mean something?*

I begin the improbable meeting: "Davidson, explain, please!"

Explain he does, with a spellbinding chronology:

"Joe, I arrived in Rochester on Christmas Eve. I had planned to pay you a surprise visit on the day after Christmas. In the wee hours of Christmas, after settling in my hotel room, I decided for no particular reason to walk with the wind along the River Medway. I made my way to the top of a hill overlooking a wild tributary that intersected and fed the river. With the bashful moon at my back, I saw something speeding downstream.

Whatever it was must have just tumbled over the weir that spanned the tributary. It was about to reach the river, which would carry it to the lowlands and the bay. I came to realize the object was a person, frantically resisting the water's undertow. I recalled the time at school when I dove to save *you* from drowning. I rushed to the bilious stream, dove in, and struggled to reach who turned out to be young Haywood. Just before he entered the river, I secured my arm around his neck and swam one-armed through the mighty, cold water to the opposite bank.

"The wind howled. The sky was pitch-dark, except when the frustrated moon could peek through the racing clouds that had just begun to heap rain across the countryside. During a brief period of faint light, I spotted a thick, sturdy bush against a hill. I carried the flaccid, almost lifeless body over my left shoulder toward the hill. *The bush will shield us from the wind,* I thought. I laid Haywood down behind the bush and looked around. There it was – a cave, long since abandoned.

"I carried Haywood inside. I saw the outlines of walls and some of the dirt floor, under fitful moon rays sneaking through cracks in the stone ceiling. There was a straw bed on the ground. I gently laid him onto it, face up, and waited for more light, which finally came and revealed something dark and viscous on the straw. I turned him on his side to determine its origin. There was blood, not fully congealed, around a nasty gash on the back of his head. I compressed my folded kerchief against the wound and tied it in place with a sturdy strand of straw.

"Haywood's eyes were barely open. I loosened his collar and saw an uninterrupted abrasion around the front and sides of his neck. *Someone tried to strangle this boy!* I wrung the water out of my coat, which I then placed under his head. I shifted him on his side. He lay, motionless and mute, for two hours. I listened to his heart and took his pulse every quarter hour. As the time passed, his heartbeat and pulse became stronger.

"By daybreak, the wind and rain were gone. Near death when I brought him into the cave, the resilient 'callant' [his dark red hair and ruddy complexion implied Scottish roots] had regained consciousness. Bleary sunlight found his pleasant face and gave it a healthy glow. Somehow, Haywood had survived.

"I told him to lie still whilst I went into town to get food; water; a blanket; vinegar, which I had seen military medics apply to heal wounds; bandages; and an oil lamp. After procuring those items, I fetched some dry clothes from my suitcase.

"Back at the cave, my careworn rescuee was resting and alert. I got him into the warm clothes; cleaned the wounds on his head and neck; and gave him water and food."

Davidson turns to Haywood.

"Haywood, tell Reverend Cleary what you told me."

Stanley looks at Motilal and then turns his attention to me:

"Motilal and I had Christmas Eve dinner with my uncle at his house. We buried our differences and became friends. Since we wouldn't see each other for a fortnight, we decided after our late dinner with my uncle to don our raingear and walk through the storm to the river, where we could watch the wind skip over the water and bend the trees. We beheld Mother Nature's havoc – brutal wind and torrential, stinging rain. An hour passed, and we left for Minor Canon Row. I left Motilal at #3 and returned, weather-worn, to my uncle's house. He demanded to know why we had stayed out in the storm for so long. I screamed: 'I am a grown man and can take care of myself!' I beheld his intimidating eyes and retreated to my room. As I was taking off my raincoat before undressing for bed, something wrapped round my neck and tightened, vice-like. Unable to breathe, I worked desperately to break free. My next recollection is the raw strength of heavy, churning water as it tried to drag me down ...

"Almost unconscious, I was about to surrender to the that irresistible force, when Mr. Davidson wrapped his arm around my aching neck. That's my last recollection, until I awoke to see Mr. Davidson looking down at me. I could only stare, not too incredulously, I hoped, at his calm, compassionate face. I thought: God *sent this man to save me.*

"That's it, Reverend Cleary. My uncle tried to kill me. I don't know what more I can say."

I ask Haywood how long he remained secreted in the cave. He replies that Davidson took him from there to his Gray's Inn flat on 15 January. For seven months, he has lived there in a secreted space behind a bookshelf.

I ask my old school chum: "Haywood lives behind the bookshelf holding your collection of the Great Books?"[44]

"The bookshelf is more than home to superb literature, Joe. It's a disguised door to a room known only to me and whoever lived there before me. It has become Haywood's haven – out of Neville Walmsley's reach."

"I have to know, Haywood and Henry, why didn't you come forward right away and spare Motilal the months-long agony of being an accused murderer? Why didn't you expose Walmsley?"

Davidson explains: "We perhaps should have appeared when Motilal was formally charged; but we had to consider that Haywood, still shell-shocked, wasn't ready to face his evil, dangerous uncle in a courtroom. We were about to come forward later, until we heard that the charge was dropped. At any rate, we are exposing Walmsley *now*."

____

[44] By 1860, The Great Books of the Western World included the most influential works of philosophy, politics, religion, science, literature, and history – from *The Old Testament* to Darwin's *On the Origin of Species (*1859).

Indira adds: "Reverend Cleary, I must confess that my brother and I have known of Haywood's rescue and whereabouts for six months. We have frequently visited him at Mr. Davidson's. He has recovered fully – physically and emotionally. We all agreed to keep his survival secret until he was prepared to face his uncle. As Mr. Davidson just implied, the day of reckoning for Neville Walmsley is near."

Davidson asks: "How should we proceed, Joe?"

I pause.

"On Monday, I will invite Walmsley here for dinner. As he enters the house, we will confront him.

"Haywood and Anne, you will live here for a few days. There's a comfortable bed in the attic and another in the spare bedroom down the hallway."

Haywood prefers to stay in the attic. He has a leather satchel containing a neatly folded suit and shirt, of stiff material; a cravat; and a pair of shriveled, brown leather, boot-like shoes.

"Reverend Cleary, here is what I had on when Mr. Davidson pulled me from the river. Will you hold them as possible evidence in my uncle's prosecution?"

I agree to serve as interim evidence custodian. I take from the top drawer of the dining room hutch what I found at the weir: the gold watch with Haywood's engraved initials, its chain, and his stick-pin – surrendered to me by Mayor Raferty after the charges against Motilal were finally nolle prossed.[45]

Haywood reacts with youthful vigor.

"Wow! I thought these were lost forever!"

"This is additional evidence, Haywood. It shall be returned to you after your uncle's case is concluded."

---

[45] Nolle pros is the English form of the legal-Latin phrase, nolle prosequi, which denotes a prosecutor's decision to dismiss criminal charges.

III

Freud turned to the next marked page and read the following shocking revelation from Dean Joseph Cleary:

26 August 1861

At 10:00, I knock at Walmsley's door. Thirty seconds pass. I knock again. Still nothing. *Something is wrong*! I turn the doorknob. The door is unlocked. I walk down the hall and call out: "Neville, are you here? It's Joe Cleary." In the study, Walmsley is seated behind his desk, which faces the shuttered window. I see only the back of his head and the rear of his shoulders. His head is tilted and motionless.

"Neville, are you alright?" Silence. No movement.

I walk around his chair. His face is frozen. His jaundiced eyes are open, like those of a dead fish; and his mouth is twisted – *by remorse?* I feel his right carotid artery. There is no pulse. He is cold to the touch, but rigor mortis has not set in. He has been dead for only a couple of hours. I smell alcohol. An overturned glass is on the floor near his chair. An empty, brown-glass bottle sits conspicuously on his desk. Its label reads: 'Tincture of Opium'.[46] A sealed envelope under a crystal paperweight lies beside the bottle. Written on the envelope in blue ink is 'Reverend Joseph Cleary'. I open it and remove the note, attached hereto.

Freud shared what Walmsley had to say to Cleary ... and to the world:

26 August 1861

07:00

Dear Reverend Cleary:

At 01:30 on Christmas Day last year, under the influence of laudanum, I crept behind my nephew as he was about to undress for bed. I had my scarf, which you will find folded in the top, right-hand

---

[46] Laudanum is a tincture (mixture) of 10% opium and 90% ethanol. Opium is a toxic, addictive narcotic. Ethanol is the type of alcohol, also deleterious, found in alcoholic drinks.

desk drawer. I positioned the scarf around his neck; and, with all the strength I could muster, began to strangle him. He strained mightily to free himself. I jerked and tightened, harder and harder, until he collapsed, unconscious. His blue-tinged lips said he was dead. I found no pulse.

I loaded his fully clothed, limp body into a barrow and covered him with heavy canvas.

The streets were deserted. The wind was wailing. Under sporadic moonlight, I rolled the barrow and its human cargo to a stream flowing forcefully over the weir toward the river. I dumped my nephew's body at the weir. The back of his head struck it, and he slid over it into the current.

I saw someone in the dim moonlight at the top of the hill. I doubt he saw me. I hurried away and started back home. At daybreak, I burned the barrow and canvas and buried their ashes in the back yard under the plane tree.

I had come to hate my nephew. I was 5 ½ years older; so, we were more like rivaling siblings than uncle and nephew. Haywood was cavalier, self-centered, and disrespectful. He was spoiled by his mother, my sister. I was pathologically jealous of him.

I am haunted by memories of our family's ill-fated return trip to London from Dover in 1855. Haywood, his parents, and I had taken the train to Dover to visit Mr. Stanley's friend, Peter Darwin, to reduce to writing their arrangement of the marriage, five years hence, between Haywood and one of Darwin's daughters, Anne Elizabeth, then only 12. She seemed more like a matured 15, Haywood's age. I remember her simple, sophisticated beauty – an uncommon quality in such a young girl.

Just outside of London, our train derailed. Haywood's parents were killed. I was critically injured and took a year to recover. Somehow, Haywood was unharmed. There is no rhyme or reason to his escaping grave injury or death. Since that awful day, I always have thought of him as a wizard – a Druid.

In 1856, still recovering from my injury, I took residence in Rochester and, not quite 22, assumed my position at the cathedral. Intense, chronic pain from my punctured lung and fractured pelvis got the better of me. I'm sure you have noticed my limp, slight as it is. I began to smoke opium to ease the agony. The drug relieved the physical pain, but it brought excruciating mental anguish. Opium starved my judgement and nourished my inner demons. I led a double life: the even-tempered, respected church figure and the fearsome, evil abuser of those whom I should have treated respectfully.

I detested Haywood all the more because he was engaged to Anne Elizabeth, with whom I was (or thought I was) madly in love. My love for her wasn't love at all. It was pure lust, the animalistic emotion born of opium.

I am deeply sorry, not only for killing my nephew, but also for so cruelly contriving false evidence against Motilal Patel, a decent, innocent person, and for being so abusive to Anne, who deserved favour and compassion.

Rue and guilt consume me, and I *must* accept responsibility for my addiction and my evil actions. There is no longer a place for me in the temporal world. My time here is over. For so long, I have lived by opium. I deserve to die by it.

Reverend Cleary, I am confessing to you because you guided me toward redemption. At last, I have chosen decency and right reason over evil and insanity. You have rescued my soul from Hell. I am eternally grateful.

God, please forgive me, who has sinned so egregiously.

Please read this letter to Motilal and his sister, and to Anne. Haywood will hear my words from Heaven.

God bless you, Reverend Cleary. I leave you with a simple plea: Will you preside at my funeral and burial?

Yours in Christ,
Neville Walmsley

Freud put down the letter, took off his spectacles, and wiped away a tear.

"This is the most heartfelt suicide note I have ever read. Notice the penmanship. It is unhurried, benign, and rhythmic– not the hasty, convulsive longhand in Walmsley's diary. The ink is merciful blue, not the sadistic black fluid pressured onto helpless pages. The person who wrote *this* note is not he who (a) tried to murder his nephew; (b) lusted after his pupil; and (c) slandered and framed young Motilal.

"By the time of this remarkable penitence, Walmsley's id, ego, and superego are in harmony. When he died, Walmsley was beside Cleary on the morality continuum.

"If one believes in atonement in its biblical context, he'll find it in this confession, which confirms the story's major theme: redemption.

<h1 style="text-align:center">IV</h1>

Freud went to the next ribbon-marked pages:

26 August 1861 (Continued)

I call the coroner, who surveys
the scene as he interviews me. He takes
into custody the suicide note, laudanum
bottle, glass, and scarf. I fully expect him
to   conclude: Neville   Walmsley
committed suicide.

At 13:00, I return home. Haywood and Anne are finishing lunch. I sit at the table and look sorrowfully at them.

"Haywood, your uncle is dead. He took his life by overdosing on laudanum. He left a suicide note."

I relate Walmsley's last words. Haywood, not at all the cocky, indifferent young adult I once knew, sobs and says: "He died believing he killed me."

Anne is equally sad.

"I was deathly afraid of him. I saw him as an incorrigible monster. I'm so happy he died a repentant soul."

I telegraph Motilal, Indira, and Davidson, who are in London, and apprise them of what happened. They were about to return to Rochester for the Walmsley confrontation, now obviated. They insist on coming anyway. I think I know why.

Freud looked upward, to The Place he believed Cleary had gone.

"I think *I* know why, as well, Reverend Cleary. I, too, see blooming romances: Haywood and Indira, and Motilal and Anne.

"Who has figured out what those relationships have in common?"

C. S. and Haywood raised their hands in unison.

"Well," said Freud, "let's have your thoughts in writing."

They wrote on cards and passed them to Freud.

C. S.: "East and West meet and cherish each other."

Haywood of Oxford: "An assimilation of cultures."

Freud shared their responses and commented:

"Your autonomous, congruent conclusions remind me of Margaret's and my *Drood* analyses. Granted, Margaret had read my id-ego-superego theory. That said, she still had to apply it to the characters; and she did so exactly as I have done, on her own. Conclusions drawn independently of each other are valid deductions.

"So, yes. The Haywood-Indira and Motilal-Anne relationships symbolize a *Drood* sub-theme: East and West *can* assimilate. If one from the Orient moves to the Occident, he must concede to Occidental culture. Likewise, if someone from the West emigrates to the East, he must accept Eastern norms, mores, and values. At the same time, one should not forsake his roots and renounce the culture of his native country when he pledges allegiance to the flag of his adoptive homeland."

"On to Reverend Cleary's next entry:

29 August 1861

Neville Walmsley's requiem is forlorn, despite the uplifting, supernal organ music. The crowded, sombre service is attended by his nephew, the Patel twins, Anne Darwin, and much of the cathedral's forgiving congregation. On the way to the cemetery, I notice the quick-lime pile, a mound of caustic substance that would dissolve anything it touched. I pray silently in its direction: "Lord God, eat away the sins of Neville Walmsley just as the quick-lime would consume his bones."

Standing at the grave is stolid Leicester Smythe,[47] the stonemason. The marker, carved in deep letters by Smythe, simply reads:

Neville Walmsley

1835-1861

Choirmaster

1856-1861

"That is enough reading for today.

---

[47] Stoney Durdles.

"Jeremy, I think everyone will welcome a day of rest. Let's take tomorrow off and resume on Monday."

I wondered how many data points we had accumulated and how many more remained. *When will the parallel lines meet?*

V

<u>20 December 1925 (Sunday)</u>.

Freud remained in our boarding house all day. Haywood, C. S., and I walked the streets of Rochester. When evening arrived, Haywood and I bid C. S. goodbye and proceeded to Rochester Cathedral.

"Not so fast! I'm coming with you!"

Our conflicted friend was reassessing his religious sentiment.

CHAPTER 9

RESURRECTION

I hope that real love and truth are
stronger in the end than any evil or
misfortune in the world.

Charles Dickens
David Copperfield
1860

<u>21 December 1925</u>.

I

Freud continued reading from Cleary's *Remembrance*.

23 November 1861

Today, I preside over the joint
marriages of two vibrant young couples
in Rochester Cathedral.

Two days before the wedding, I
witnessed a tender interaction between
Haywood and Motilal. I had invited them,
their future wives, and the wedding party
to a prenuptial dinner in #3 Minor Canon
Row.

142

After dinner, Haywood took from his pocket a diamond and ruby ring. He handed it to Motilal and said: "This wedding ring belonged to Anne's mother. Her father took it from her finger after she tragically drowned. Just before he died, he left it with Mr. Blair, who gave it to me to place on Anne's finger. When we cancelled our engagement, I was bound to return the ring to Mr. Blair. Before I could do so, cruel fate took me to the weir. The angels, thank God, intervened and sent Mr. Davidson to my rescue. He saved me from drowning, nursed me back to health, and gave me a safe place to stay. In his Gray's Inn flat, I saw the gentle, unshakeable love flowing between you and Anne. I knew someday you and she would marry. This ring was meant for *her*; and God wants *you* to slip it onto her finger in Rochester Cathedral."

Mr. Blair rose, walked to Haywood, and embraced him. Then, he returned to his seat and tried in vain to swallow the lump in his throat.

Anne sobbed, kissed her erstwhile beau, and said: "Woody, I shall forever remember this day; and I shall always love you as my dearest friend. I'll *never* forget you, Woody."

Motilal, who had come to love and respect his former foe, reached into his own pocket and produced a modest gold band set with a single blue sapphire.

"Woody, this was my dear mum's ring meant to be Indira's wedding band. Just as God wanted Anne to have the ring of her departed mother, He chose *you* to place this blessed sapphire on Indira's finger."

Motilal gave the symbol of his parent's love for each other to his friend and future brother-in-law. Indira hugged her husband-to-be, held his hand, and said: "Woody, I believe with all my heart, when she reached Heaven and looked down into her little twins' sad eyes, my mother knew this beautiful day would come."

I had grown quite fond of Haywood Stanley, who, with loving

Anne, had lived with me since 23 August. During those three months, their relationship evolved into a wholesome union, much like the unbreakable bond between Motilal and Indira.

I was glad that my four dear, young friends had found happiness. Still, I was sad that Haywood and Anne would leave Minor Canon Row.

Davidson proposed a toast:

"To him who has helped so many find their way in this troubled world. To *you*, Joe, who gave respite to Haywood and Anne and made the twins from Ceylon feel welcome and accepted in this lonely town, so far away from their roots; *and*, who cleansed the defiled soul of Neville Walmsley. You pointed that corrupted sinner to salvation. Thanks to you, Heaven is within his reach, if he's not already there.

"Don't be sorry as your boarders, whom you hold so dear, prepare to leave for Highclere Castle to join Motilal and Indira. It's a vast estate, with farmland needing the care and supervision of competent, able-bodied men like Haywood and Motilal. The house itself is huge and cries for the woman's touch that Anne and Indira can give it.

"You, my friend, may visit us *anytime,* and we will come often to Rochester to see you."

"Well," said Freud, "Reverend Cleary has given us another data point: the ring that Stanley had in his vest pocket when his uncle threw him into the water – to be dragged out to sea."

He read further.

12 April 1866

Woody pays one of his frequent visits. I had prepared the attic for his five-day stay.

Reminiscences about his mysterious disappearance and his uncle's shocking suicide still preoccupy him. He wants very much to put behind him the frightful Christmas of 1860.

Woody and Indira are expecting their first child in June. The Stanley surname would be forever linked to murder, suicide, and

opium. They decide to bury Stanley and
take a new family name for the sake of
their child. I walk with him to the
courthouse to file a 'Petition for Change
of Name'.

Freud came to the page marked with the last blue ribbon, attached to its upper right-hand corner. I wondered why this ribbon was positioned differently than the others, which were tucked in the journal's inner margins.

A curious, unexpected request: "Sig, may I read to the group Cleary's remaining post?"

Freud was not at all surprised. He paused ever so briefly before asking, "Why, Haywood?"

"I dreamt last night that *you* suggested I should."

With an all-knowing smile, Sig handed over to the Dickens scholar the startling account that would shock him to his core.

I stared discreetly at the Roundtrees. With sympathetic smiles, they looked at Haywood and sat stone-silent. They and Freud knew very well what was to come next. Freud knew through pure deduction. The Roundtrees knew because, as C. S., Haywood, and I would learn, they had read, some time ago, *everything* that came out of the wardrobe.

Freud: "Haywood, take us to the next data point."

The man whom Destiny chose to read the last marked page shared the entry that would break the Canon Code:

17 April 1866

I walk with Woody to the courthouse. The matter on the court docket reads:

"In Re Haywood Stanley, No. 66-456
Petition for Change of Name"

The hearing is a perfunctory proceeding. Woody is sworn in by the clerk and confirms to the court and the state solicitor that he is changing his surname of his own free will for appropriate familial reasons, which he stated in detail.

With the state solicitor's consent, the magistrate grants the petition and reads into the record the following judgement:

"In the Matter of Haywood Stanley, case number 66-456 on the docket of the Magistrate Court, City of Rochester, Kent: Considering the petitioner's sworn testimony, which the Court deems credible, and concluding that there is no just cause to deny the relief prayed for,

IT IS ORDERED, ADJUDGED, AND DECREED that the name of HAYWOOD STANLEY be, and the same is hereby formally and legally changed to HAYWOOD TOWNES CHAMBERS.

JUDGEMENT READ, RENDERED, AND SIGNED on this 17th day of April in the year of our Lord 1866.

[The magistrate signs the judgement and affixes the court seal over his signature.]

Freud's parallel lines were parallel no longer. They bent to become conjoined at both ends. My mind's eye saw what that foresightful genius said would happen all along.

He got up, gently placed his hands on the slumping shoulders of stupefied Haywood Townes Chambers Jr., and said: "Yes, Haywood, your father was Haywood Stanley, the young man to whom Dickens gave the fictitious name Edwin Drood … the man whom you never knew as Haywood Stanley. *You* are the resurrection of Edwin Drood!

Well, well, well! Resurrection! Sig, have you made the leap to Christianity? I kept my thoughts to myself, as I battled incredulity over the jaw-dropping revelation that my mentor is the progeny of the eponymous main character in Charles Dickens's final and best effort.

Freud: "This crowning data point establishes indisputably that *The Mystery of Edwin Drood* is *not* fiction. The scion of Edwin Drood is here in the flesh, before our very eyes. Dickens left *two* mysteries. The presumptive mystery entails the fate of Edwin Drood. Until now, no one, except for the keepers of the secrets in #3 Minor Canon Row, knew that *Drood* is about actual events in the lives of real people, whose identities Dickens shielded with fictional names. He would disclose who they were in the concluding chapters."

Freud was *so* much like Holmes. From the beginning, he knew intuitively what we would find in the attic. More than anything else, his *imagination* took us to Gad's Hill Place and #3 Minor Canon Row.

I thought about his most notable contemporary, who also would alter the course of history – Albert Einstein,[48] the scientific wizard who postulated E=mc2. Many have sought to debunk that Promethean equation, which posits that energy and matter are different forms of the same thing: energy is matter multiplied by the speed of light squared. Einstein's mathematical formula, acted out at the subatomic level in the atomic bomb, would result in the devastation the world would see in Hiroshima and Nagasaki. His unparalleled mastery of mathematics and physics, by itself, would not have yielded E=mc2, as much the result of his *imagination* as it is of his

---

[48] Albert Einstein (1879-1955) was the theoretical physicist whose famous 1905 equation led to the development of the atomic bomb, the inconceivably explosive weapon that decimated its targets and forced Japan's surrender in World War II.

mathematical/scientific genius. So it is with Freud. His deductive/inductive reasoning skills, combined with his potent imagination, would take us from #3 Minor Canon Row to our (and Dickens's) final destination, the place where ideation and fact became one.

Freud noticed my old teacher's return to normalcy.

"Haywood, are you ready for the next disclosure?"

"Well, now you may call me Woody! After all we've been through, I'm ready for *anything*!"

Clearly, Haywood was fine. His welcome, innocent levity drew chuckles.

Freud smiled and motioned to Roundtree.

"Jeremy, it's time for some cognac. Don't you agree?"

"Lovely idea, Sig."

[Freud's suggestion of a recess was a measured move.]

As we went downstairs, I placed my hand on Haywood's shoulder and jokingly asked: "Woody, are you steady enough?"

"Is the Pope Catholic?"

I playfully shoved him.

"I'll take your rhetorical response as a resounding *Yes*!"

Margaret brought the brandy, which she had supplemented with firm cheese slices and thin biscuits.

Haywood: "Before the next disclosure, which no doubt is a dividend to all that we have discovered, I have a question."

Freud: "You're wondering why your father chose as his new middle and surname Townes and Chambers. I'm afraid that's a mystery to be solved on another day."

I offered a toast: "Hear! Hear! That's our next project!

[Light-hearted laughter amidst sips of throat-warming brandy]

Freud: "Now, for what Haywood refers to as the 'dividend'.

"Haywood, do you remember what you said a few days ago about the man on the wall?"

"Yes, Sig. I said the painter's strokes are 'familiar'. I had seen brushmarks like those before."

Freud: "Jeremy, can you take it down?"

Roundtree complied.

Haywood: "Sig, you know what's inscribed on the back of the painting, don't you?"

"I *think* I do."

The obliging minor canon, assisted by his daughter, lifted Dickens from his exclusive place on the wall and turned him around. There it was, at the framing's lower right corner: 'H.T.C.'

Freud turned to Haywood.

"H. T. C. … Haywood Townes Chambers – *ne'* Haywood Stanley, the contrite young man whom Dickens called Edwin Drood, is the artist. When he was Rosa's caddish future husband, he painted her in a most careless, sloppy way. *This* rendering of Dickens, done some eight years later, is the brilliant, deliberate work of a respectful virtuoso."

Roundtree: "Woody, your dad was visiting Dean Cleary in Minor Canon Row on the day Dickens first appeared here, on 11 October 1867. You were just over a year old. He was in the attic, applying the finishing touches to his new painting of Anne, as she watched him from behind. He wanted to redeem himself for his previous attempt, which Sig aptly called 'a travesty'.

"Dickens entered the attic with Reverend Cleary, who introduced him to the stern, young artist and his elegant subject, both of whom he would read about in the documents awaiting him in the wardrobe. Dickens fell in love with the just-completed portrait of the lovely, uncorrupted girl and asked the person whom the world knows as Edwin Drood to paint him in the same way, after his return from his American book and reading tour, seven months hence.

"The 1868 visitors' ledgers have Haywood Chambers Sr. here on four of the days when Dickens went to the attic to examine everything in the wardrobe. On those days, after Dickens had finished his research, your father drew, as his distinguished subject posed, the sketches that underlay this stunning piece of art.

"Woody, you became the world's leading Dickens expert because Haywood Sr. taught you so many things about the illustrious figure whom he had met and befriended. For whatever reason, he never mentioned to you his meetings with him in #3 Minor Canon Row. He never revealed that he had produced Charles Dickens on canvas."

Haywood remembered! [He looked upward and spoke more to himself than to us.]

"My God! The *brushstrokes*! I just realized that it is my *dad* who painted the fabulous piece that I have long admired at the Christ Church Picture Gallery – the endearing image of an untainted, dainty, bonny lass with lustrous brown hair, a porcelain-smooth face, and deep blue eyes. She is the girl whom Dickens had painted with words – the comely fiancée of Edwin Drood – Rosa Bud, whom we now know as Anne Darwin Patel.

"I always get up close to her. She stares innocently from her gold frame. When I look into her eyes, they follow mine. She smiles; and, for a moment, she comes alive, just as Mona Lisa does from her resting place at the Louvre whenever one is alone with her.

"The lower right-hand corner only shows '1867'. The plaque beneath the painting simply reads: 'Portrait of a Young Woman'. Artist unknown'. Haywood Townes Chambers anonymously graced Anne, whom he had treated so crudely, with that redemptive painting, so exceptional that the Christ Church Picture Gallery has displayed it for the last seven years.

"My father died five years ago, two years after my mother, to whom Dickens had given the fictitious name Helena Landless. Soon after she died, he came to live with me in Oxford. When he passed away, I had no idea that *he* was the unnamed artist behind 'Portrait of a Young Woman'. *My dad* gave that marvelous painting to the Picture Gallery. The young woman is Rosa Bud … sorry … Anne Darwin Patel! I'll be damned!'"

Haywood's soliloquy ended. He addressed us directly.

"In my humble opinion, the paintings of Dickens and the Young Woman are the works of a gifted artist who, absent any structured training, rivaled da Vinci and Montorfano.[49] He conveyed his subjects' humanity as only a maestro could. His hand and eye were as acute as a camera and its lens. He painted as exquisitely as Dickens wrote."

Roundtree revealed something further.

"Haywood, Reverend Cleary's subsequent entries, which everyone will see presently, tell us that, in May, June, July, and August 1868, when you were two years old, your parents came to spend a few days. You remained back at Highclere with Motilal and Anne. Your father wanted to do for Dickens what he had done for Anne. He scheduled him to sit on various days for sketches.[50] There was one session in May, two in June, and one in July. He finished drawing on 30 July, the date of Dickens's penultimate visit to Minor Canon Row. He stayed a week in August, alone in the attic, brush in hand – painting away.

"When he was done, he summoned Cleary and uncovered what you see before us. The minor canon was awestruck. He wrote in his *Remembrance*: 'The fresh paint glistened in the sun's light.'

---

[49] Leonardo da Vinci (1452-1519) is best known for his redoubtable portrayal of *The Last Supper* (1498) and for his classic achievement, *The Mona Lisa* (1503-1506).

Donato Montorfano (1460-1503) painted *The Crucifixion* (1495), the crucified bodies of Christ and the two thieves who perished with Him. A dense crowd surrounds the three tortured men as they are dying on their crosses. Da Vinci supplemented Montorfano's masterpiece with additional figures in the crowd.

[50] Chambers Sr. mastered the art of sketching on canvas – the foundation for good oil painting.

"Cleary and your parents invited Dickens to see himself, in this gilded frame, on 25 August 1868, his final visit. He wept as he saw his image – an exhausted, aging man resigned to his imminent death but fully satisfied with the exemplary life he had led. He asked your father to name his price. 'I am not a trained artist,' your father said. 'The painting is yours, gratis. Having you as a friend is the highest honour.'

"Dickens smiled as the bighearted prodigy offered his hand.

'This place has been so kind to me. I shall draw upon my time here to compose my swan song – an explosive mystery involving, among others, you three who stand before me. It will be unlike any story I have written. I won't live long enough to finish it. God will choose someone else to see it to fruition. I want you to hang me somewhere in this place that I shall call Minor Canon Corner and, later, #3 Minor Canon Row.'

"He hugged your parents and bade them farewell. Reverend Cleary accompanied him down the stairs, from the serene room that the tearful gentleman had seen for the last time, to the front door. Before departing, he shared his plan: 'Next year, I shall begin drafting a *true* chronology about a young man who, on Christmas morning in 1860, disappeared near the River Medway and was presumed drowned – the prodigious lad who painted my craggy face and weary body, which is ready to surrender to what I believe is a terminal illness. You shall know the *whole* story, Reverend Cleary. It's in the wardrobe. *You*, like each of the youngsters in the attic, are integral to its plots and themes. All who will appear with fictitious names in the first six or so installments, likely to be published before or shortly after I die, will see that the serial is about *them* and everything they experienced just before and for months after Haywood's disappearance. The first installment is tentatively planned for publication in April 1870. Kind Sir, will you, about a month before then, assemble those true-life players and beseech them to remain silent about their identities and their roles as they read the early chapters? I will send you a list of their names and last known whereabouts. Let them know I will leave it to those favoured by God to reveal the rest of this genuine piece of history.'

"Cleary looked at the melancholy man through blurry eyes.

'Sir, have you decided on a title?'

'Not yet. I'll settle on one before I begin to write.'

"The minor canon pledged to bring together all the listed characters and pass along to them the plea by him whom they all knew of – the man who wanted to make them participants in a new art form.

"Dickens shook his host's hand and said in a sad, yet happy, way: 'Thank you, Reverend Cleary. Thank you from the bottom of my heart.' He backed away, waved farewell, turned around, and melted into the twilight.

"On 4 March 1870, every living *Drood* character gathered in the two front pews at Rochester Cathedral. (Richard Myerscough, Leicester Smythe, and Miss Meade had died.) Haywood, Indira, Motilal, and Anne already knew about Dickens's plan, because Cleary had told them about it soon after his final visit to #3 in 1868. They sat passively as Cleary informed the rest of his audience of the upcoming story involving the incident at the weir and all its ramifications – a story about *all of them*. He announced that Dickens expected to die before he finished and would rely on those inspired by God to bring it to conclusion, whilst revealing the actual identities of its true-life characters. They all promised to say nothing unless and until the story was finished by the chosen ones, whenever that might be."

Freud: "Well, Jeremy, I don't need to read the rest of what the late Reverend Cleary had to say. You just summarized it flawlessly."

The Roundtrees rehung the great man at his privileged place on the wall.

II

Freud reminded us there was more to be done: loose ends to tie up. *Are there* more *surprises?*

"To sum up: We have lined up all the connecting blocks. Moreover, we saw what no one else ever imagined: *The Mystery of Edwin Drood* is, in *every* aspect, *true*. Dickens left clues of its factuality at Gad's Hill Place – cues for someone to take on his way to the attic in #3 Minor Canon Row.

"Soon after we left Gad's Hill, I redacted from the 1855 *Daily News* train wreck report the Stanley and Walmsley names and chose to reveal this clipping at the right time, which is now. [Freud produced the section of the 1855 story he had clandestinely clipped and removed from the newspaper section given to him by Nigel Lloyd.]

"Think of this strip of newspaper as the ribbon around the *Edwin Drood* package."

"You took down at Gad's Hill School the names of Neal Stanley, Indira Walmsley Stanley, Haywood Stanley, and Neville Walmsley, didn't you? It's the list you gave to Nigel Lloyd, isn't it?"

"Yes, Buck. I copied those four names. I saw a nexus amongst them. Stanley's incomprehensible, injury-free survival was, simply stated, unworldly. Yes, he reminded me of the transcendent Celtic priests: the 'Druids'. Hence, the name 'Drood'.

"I'll tape this section back onto the article this evening, when we are at our rooms."

"Why did you cut it out?"

"Buck, the capital rule of investigation is: 'Don't get ahead of yourself.'"

Roundtree imparted enlightening information.

"Dickens, then living at Gad's Hill Place, took frequent walks in and around Rochester. One early fall day in 1867, as he lunched at his preferred Rochester pub, he recalled the 1865 Staplehurst train accident, which took his mind back to 1855, when another tragic train crash had been reported in *The Daily News*, where he had served earlier as editor in chief. The names Stanley and Walmsley came to mind. He followed his instinct to the cathedral cemetery, where a particular headstone grabbed his attention:

Neville Walmsley
1835-1861

Choirmaster
1856-1861

He recalled the four names he had seen listed together in the 1855 *Daily News* article: Haywood Stanley; Neville Walmsley; Indira Walmsley Stanley; and Neal Stanley – respectively, the miraculous, unscathed survivor and his three unfortunate companions seriously injured or killed in that dreadful train wreck.

"He connected the gravestone and 1855 to the well publicised story of the lad who had disappeared at the Medway weir on Christmas 1860. Dickens thought, or imagined, that everything relating to the disappearance lay at the house of Reverend Joseph Cleary, the minor canon who, according to church records, had officiated at Walmsley's funeral.

"Remember, it was on 11 October 1867, which must have been after his cemetery visit, that Dickens first appeared in #3 Minor Canon Row."

I had to ask: "Jeremy, how did you learn what you just revealed?"

"I heard it from Dickens after he introduced himself at my front door. I let Sig know about it during your first day in #3, as you, C. S., and Haywood were engaged in a side conversation with Margaret. I was about to tell you three what I had told Sig; but he stopped me and said: 'Reverend Roundtree, it's premature to tell them now.'

Freud: "Are you angry, Buck?"

I winked and mustered a few light-hearted words.

"As you have said, you didn't want us to get ahead of ourselves. I *should* be angry, but how can I be, when I know your modus operandi so well?"

Revealing his avuncular side, Freud tousled my hair. Then, the personable gentleman rewarded us yet again with his preternatural insight.

"I see what would have been Dickens's 'Afterword' as clearly as I see him on the wall. Had he lived, he would have written something like this:

Dear readers,

You by now know that *The Mystery of Edwin Drood* is *true*. In the first six installments, I disguised the real names of people and places to preserve, as long as possible, the characters' privacy.

Even if it were the purest fiction, *Drood* nonetheless would be 'true'. Often, there is more truth in fiction than there is in so-called 'reality', too frequently the upshot of specious, false-narrative journalism.

Is Christ merely a metaphor, a figment of the believer's imagination? No matter. He is regardless *real*. He is the embodiment of good and evil's worst enemy. IIc is the irreproachable *Ideal* – the Alpha and Omega, the image of the best possible moral being. No one is more 'perfect' than He who died on the Cross.

Just as Christ is 'real', so is David Copperfield, who is *I*, myself, from infancy to maturity. Scrooge, who represents the worship of money and disdain for benevolence, is light years away from 'pretend'. I can go on and on down the long list of my fictional characters who are often closer to reality than reality is to itself.

Edwin Drood, in and out of his fictional cocoon, symbolizes life in the complex, troubled, paradoxical Western world. His story is about dysfunctional people in a disordered society, set straight by adaptive, balanced players in the arena he named Cloisterham, later to become Rochester.

This story shines a light on burning, universal contradictions: right and wrong; good and evil; cowardice and bravery; honesty and deceit; love and hatred ... It reminds us of the curse of opium; the misery of psychological imprisonment; the despair born of loneliness and boredom; the resistance to cultural assimilation; the overwhelming pull of redemption; and more.

I hope every reader takes this 'story' for what it is – a lesson in how we must meet life's challenges by confronting evil, tragedy, injustice, and misfortune, whenever they rear their ugly heads.

"Dickens knew *Drood* would be his final fling, which he would not live to finish on paper. He decided to play a game of cat and mouse with his vast, hungry audience. His was a clever gambit. As he had anticipated, scores of authors would take his bait. They wrote novels, plays, and musicals – all claiming to solve the mystery. Those shallow, whimsical efforts do little justice to his Meisterstuck.[51] He chose *us*, this ring of six in #3 Minor Canon Row, to ferret out the *facts* and shout to the world: *The Mystery of Edwin Drood* **really happened** – in a slumbrous cathedral town in the London Basin – an idyllic setting of little or no moment to the rest of humanity. At the same time, this 'insignificant spot on the globe' is a microcosm of the West, with all its imperfections and virtues.

"Drood's uncivil, bigoted treatment of dark-skinned Neville Landless affirms the West's irrational, race-based prejudice. Neville's

---

[51] Crowning achievement; *chef d'oeuvre*.

initial illogical animus toward Crisparkle illustrates the Orient's hardened insularity and its hostility to the Occidental world, a world it doesn't grasp. This clash of civilisations disappears when both sides realise that their similarities run much deeper than their differences. With the engagements and intermarriages of Neville Landless (Motilal Patel) to Rosa Bud (Anne Darwin) and Edwin Drood (Haywood Stanley/Chambers Sr.) to Helena Landless (Indira Patel), cross-cultural enmity disappears. Individualism triumphs over group-identity, the warped outlook where one sees himself, not as a unique being, but as a member of a particular race, ethnicity, religion, sex, or other group. Dickens reminds us there is only *one* race: the *human* race, begot by *one* Creator, whether He be called God, Yahweh, or Allah.

"We thus have seen the genius of Charles Dickens, the autodidact who teaches the world lessons about human nature and human interaction just as Shakespeare did centuries before.[52] Dickens is Shakespeare in prose. He explains the human condition by describing and analysing the thoughts and behaviour of those who interact in complex societies.

"The man was multi-gifted. He was a sage and a moralist with deeply held philosophic beliefs rooted in universal truths. He had what only a very few possessed: extraordinary powers of observation; Einsteinian/Holmesian imagination; and nonpareil descriptive skill. He painted vivid pictures with florid words. His canvas was the parchment

---

[52] William Shakespeare (1564-1616), the English poet and playwright, is perhaps the most admired writer in Western literature.

he wrote on; his brush was his quill. He was a realist, who wrote about what he *saw* – stark *reality*. His stories were never driven by idealised versions of the life he knew.

"So, my lettered colleagues, we see that Dickens the novelist was never a writer of pure fiction. Far from it. He alone elevated classic Victorian fiction to another, distant dimension, as I shall explain.

"Like many of his noted contemporaries, he blended fact and fiction by drawing on his own rich and sometimes tragic life experiences to create reality-based stories wrapped in fiction. *David Copperfield* is essentially autobiographical. *Martin Chuzzlewit*[53] is in no sense an invention. It's a narrative, formatted as a novel – by and large about Dickens's first trip to America, his challenging times there, and his disappointment in the still nascent country that he idealistically thought would be utopic. Those two works and many others owe as much to the true adventures of Charles Dickens as they do to his uncanny imagination.

"With Drood, he takes classic Victorian 'quasi-fiction' a huge step further. There was to be nothing chimerical about the life and times of Edwin Drood. Creative Charles, the Victorian Renaissance/Enlightenment man, would do much more than tell a story. He had in mind a new genre: the pivot from ostensible fiction to hard fact, whilst preserving plot, theme, and all the literary devices theretofore reserved for conventional works of fiction."

---

[53] *Martin Chuzzlewit* (1844) was written on the heels of Dickens's first visit to America in 1842.

It was only appropriate that Haywood Townes Chambers Jr. should comment on what the sagacious Wiener[54] just said.

"Sig, your analyses are, as always, squarely on target, and you are so right that he chose *us* to finish his final effort. Do you believe we were predestined to do what we did? Predestination is a Christian doctrine, and you are an atheist."

"Predestination is incompatible with the atheistic notion that things happen through blind, godless chance. But, Woody, given everything we have seen over the last nine days, even a hidebound atheist has to admit: Providence played a hand in the revelations at Gad's Hill, the weir, the cave, and #3 Minor Canon Row."

"Well, what is Providence?"

"I don't know, *yet*."

The time was ripe for me to chime in.

"Sig, I was awestruck when you called Woody 'the resurrection of Edwin Drood'. I thought that you quite possibly were conceding to Christianity,[55] or, at least, admitting to its plausibility."

"Am I, Buck? We'll have to wait and see."

C. S. offered a taste of Latin.

"Annuit Coeptis comes to mind. 'God has favored our undertaking."

---

[54] Freud was a 'Wiener' – one from Vienna.

[55] The Resurrection of Jesus Christ is the defining doctrine of Christianity.

III

Roundtree treated us to a celebratory dinner at Tiny Tim's,[56] a fine restaurant very near the cathedral, where our *'groupe de six'* would enjoy delicious food, fine spirits, and pleasant company.

---

[56] Jeremy must have had in mind Tiny Tim, the sick, struggling, young indigent in Dickens's immortal novella, *A Christmas Carol* (1843). Tim symbolizes the misery of Victorian England's poor. Roundtree, like all of his predecessors, often tended to the sick and poor in Rochester.

CHAPTER 10

THE SPIRITUALIST AND OPIUM

…Why can't so many of us see that

spiritualism and science are one? That

bodies evolve and souls evolve, and the

universe is a fluid place that marries

them both in a wonderful package called

a human being. What's wrong with that

idea?

Garth Stein[57]

There were opium dens where one could

buy oblivion, dens of horror where the

memory of old sins could be destroyed

by the madness of sins that were new.

Oscar Wilde
The Picture of Dorian Gray[58]

---

[57] Garth Stein (b. 1964) is an American author, playwright, film maker, and spiritualist.

Arthur Conan Doyle (1859-1930) was a Christian Spiritualist, one who believes in a place outside the physical world. We are spirit before birth, spirit within our physical bodies, and spirit after death. Doyle believed that spirits in the spiritual world and those in living bodies on Earth could communicate.

[58] *The Picture of Dorian Gray* (1890) is a Gothic novel written by Oscar Wilde (1854-1900), an Irish-born Englishman who was mainly a poet and playwright; but he is best known for his only novel.

<u>22 December 1925</u>.

I

We began our final session in #3. As usual, Freud steered.

"Again, the evidence is plotted along two non-Euclidian parallel lines – continua that will intersect at their opposite poles. I plotted everything last night, when you were asleep:

o____o

Gad's Hill/Rochester   #3 Minor Canon Row

**********canon code card   *****Attic
**********newspaper articles   *****Wardrobe
**********the name change
*****Cleary's letter and codicil   *****Walmsley diary entries
******weir and cave   *****Cleary's *Remembrance*
                               *****Walmsley's suicide note

                               ****Painting of Rosa
                               ****Painting of Anne
                               ****Dickens portrait
                       ***Stanley's letter to Walmsley
                               ***Items in boxes
                                     ***The ring

DROOD'S FATE   **TRUE STORY**

o____o

Drood   Jasper
**'Mystery'   **Cloisterham
**Druid   **Encounter at
**Drood's words to Jasper   Nuns' House
   about his father   Jasper/Rosa

169

"Picture that (a) the top line, heavily weighted at both poles, has descended markedly from both ends; and (b) the bottom line, bearing relatively little weight at either pole, has ascended slightly from its ends. So, the lines have converged: on the left at **Drood's Fate** and on the right to reveal that (a) real-life, **True-Story** people are caught up in intrigue and sin, and (b) then experience the healing effect of redemption."

I complimented Freud on his inventive configuration and added: "Yes, Sig. The lines now form a neatly tied, **True-Story** ribbon.

II

C. S. was never one to leave a stone unturned.

"We have forgotten Princess Puffer and Dick Datchery."

Freud was assuring.

"No, C. S. My friend looked into Puffer and Datchery. I neglected to include them ... because they're not indispensable to solving the mystery. [momentary pause] On second thought, perhaps I should have included Puffer."

"Who is your friend?"

"His name is Sir James George Frazer,[59] a social anthropologist from Cambridge. Like me, he's a Dickens aficionado who is fascinated by the *Drood* mystique. As we 'literary

---

[59] Sir James George Frazer (1854-1941) was a Scottish social anthropologist who posited that human understanding advanced across three phases: primitive magic, replaced by religion, replaced by science.

anthropologists' were unearthing the 'artifacts' in the wardrobe, Sir James discovered that Puffer was Theresa Cotton, the infamous owner of the Whitechapel opium den patronized by Jack Jasper. My friend found at the British Library the visitors' logs for London's 'dens of horror'. From 1856 to 1861, Walmsley visited Cotton's den 157 times.

"Puffer, now Cotton, set out to extort Jasper, now Walmsley, who, in his opioid stupor, had divulged to her his intention to murder his nephew. We see her at the end of Serial Number 6 – lurking in the shadows of Rochester Cathedral, shaking an angry fist at him.

"Opium's role in the final session between Puffer and Jasper brings to mind something that had intrigued Dickens for quite some time: *mesmerism*. He attended several demonstrations on the subject and became a staunch advocate of that widely discussed hypnotic process, developed by Franz Mesmer, an 18th-19th-century Austrian physician. Dickens actually practised it. His most notable experience with the seductive technique occurred in 1844. A lady named Augusta de la Rue suffered from severe, intractable anxiety, a puzzling condition that caused pronounced facial tics and spasms. Dickens 'mesmerized' the bewildered lady frequently over a period of months. He didn't cure her, but she experienced some relief. Their sessions had evolved into a psychotherapist/patient relationship, a dynamic unique in the mid-19th century.

"Like Dickens, I studied mesmerism, the precursor to hypnosis, a method intrinsic to psychoanalysis. Recall what I said days ago: 'Dickens was Freudian pre-Freud.' The unwonted Victorian chap was astonishing, for sure. He was a man far ahead of his time.

"I introduce mesmerism ..."

Haywood cut in.

"You bring up mesmerism because the last meeting between Puffer and Jasper illustrates it. *Opium* mesmerized Jasper. Puffer was cunning enough to realise he was in a hypnotic state and would bring to light things buried in his dark mind. In a crude way, Puffer became, for a few fleeting moments, a Freudian psychoanalyst."

Freud: "*Volltreffer*, Professor Chambers! The Dickens authority took the words from my mouth. You're so right, Woody. Puffer is not the 'mesmerist', as so many so-called experts claim. O*pium* is. It, with a gentle hand from Puffer, coerced Jasper to admit his guilt. Opium – the elixir of deceit that became, in the case of Jasper, the potion of truth. That's quite a contradiction, isn't it?

"Likewise, that ruinous narcotic, *not* Jasper, had induced the 'hypnotic' states that shattered the inhibitions of Edwin and Neville and forced heir hot-tempered confrontation at Jasper's house.

"Sir James found old Rochester newspaper articles reporting that 'Madam' Cotton was found dead on 24 August 1861 in the alley abutting the cathedral. She died of an opium overdose. Her rigid hand clutched an empty brown bottle, much like the vessel found on Walmsley's desk next to his suicide note. The label read: 'Laudanum ... Poison'. Its moist cork lay on the ground against Cotton's corpse. The wretched woman died before she could reveal the true nature of her homicidal customer, whom she viscerally hated.

"Sir James determined that Dick Datchery was Edward Cooke, a retired London inspector and private eye. He was hired by Robin Blair,

Dickens's Mr. Grewgious, to surveil Walmsley, an imminent threat to his ward, Anne, i.e., Rosa. It is Cooke who discovered Theresa Cotton's opium-polluted body. His employment ended upon Walmsley's death on 26 August 1861.

"I have planned dinner for tomorrow evening at the Crown and Anchor, where I shall introduce everyone to Sir James, who will tell you more about his findings in London and Rochester."

"Shall we tell your friend all about *our* findings at Gad's Hill, the weir, the cave, and #3 Minor Canon Row?"

"He already knows, C. S. I have been notifying him continually of our adventures."

"When, pray tell, have you been doing *that*?"

"When you, Haywood, and Buck were fast asleep during the wee hours of the mornings at our *pied-a-terre*. "

There was a sad, reflective pause that concerned me.

"Sig, what's troubling you?"

"We have been reminded of the destructive influence of opium on both mind and body. We saw what the heartless narcotic did to Neville Walmsley, Theresa Cotton, and even to Mrs. Roundtree, a sophisticated lady of faith. Dickens himself took laudanum for pain. The combination of ethyl alcohol and opium might have contributed to his premature death. Well, my friends, I *myself* have used opium and cocaine to alleviate pain. I wonder: Am *I* guilty of unpardonable indiscretions?"

I placed my hand on Freud's forearm and said: "Remember *Drood's* leading theme, Sig."

He looked at me dolefully.

"Redemption – salvation from sin ... God's gift reserved for *believers*, Buck."

"My dear Dr. Freud, I believe you *will* become a believer. I believe, one day, you will feel the touch of God."

He wiped away tears and smiled.

"Thank you, Buck. You're a true friend."

<u>23 December 1925</u>.

III

Eight Dickensian stalwarts, who had addressed (or so it seemed) every aspect of an enduring mystery, sat down for dinner at the Crown & Anchor:

(1) Sigmund Freud – the peerless social/medical scientist who found the *Drood* roadmap at Gad's Hill and pieced together all the clues in and near #3 Minor Canon Row;

(2-4) C. S. Lewis, Haywood Townes Chambers Jr., and Yours Truly – the Oxford contingent who accompanied and assisted Freud during one of history's most inspired journeys;

(5-6) Dean Jeremy Roundtree and his daughter, Margaret – the residents of #3 Minor Canon Row and the trustees of all those items and documents scrupulously analysed by Dickens as he laid the foundation for our cracking the Canon Code;

(7) Sir James George Frazer – the noted anthropologist who demystified Princess Puffer and Dick Datchery; and

(8) Nigel Lloyd – the accommodating head of Gad's Hill School, where the *Drood* saga was conceived, born, and nurtured. It was he who unwittingly preserved the fragile, time-worn card with the code, the key to the treasures in #3.

IV

At midnight, after everyone else had left, we waved goodbye to the father/daughter keepers of *les clefs d'or* to the secrets in the attic at the providential place I respectfully and affectionately came to call '#3'. We parted ways, never to meet again, except through occasional correspondence via the post.

Back at our suite, Freud proposed we spend Christmas in London. He added, rather rhetorically: "Don't you think it befitting to spend a few hours on Christmas Day amongst the spirits at Westminster Abbey?"

CHAPTER 11

THE MAN BENEATH OUR FEET

I will honour Christmas in my heart and

try to keep it all the year. I will live in

the Past, the Present, and the Future. The

Spirits of all Three shall strive within

me. I will not shut out the lessons they

teach. Oh, tell me I may sponge away

the writing on this stone!

Ebenezer Scrooge
A Christmas Carol

I

<u>24 December 1925</u>.

We checked into London's Langham Hotel, where Arthur Conan Doyle[60] and Oscar Wilde[61] had met over dinner in 1889 to discuss their writings. The meeting led to Wilde's *The Picture of Dorian Gray*[62] and Doyle's *The Sign of Four*.[63]

---

[60] Arthur Conan Doyle, note 57, supra. The Scottish physician-turned-author, Sir Arthur Conan Doyle (1859-1930), created the enduring fictional detective, Sherlock Holmes, who 'really' was the forensic scientist Joseph Bell (1837-1911), who mentored Doyle, a medical student at the Edinburgh Royal Infirmary. Doyle was fascinated by Bell's sharp imagination and deductive-reasoning ability.

[61] Note 58, supra.

[62] Id.

[63] *The Sign of Four* (1890) is Conan Doyle's second novel featuring Sherlock Holmes.

At the hotel's Artesian Bar, I asked Freud: "Did Dickens coax you to Westminster Abbey?"

"Buck, as you and the others know, Dickens lies at Poet's Corner there. I need to talk to him."

"Whoah! Freud the spiritualist!"

"*I*, a Spiritualist? We'll see, Buck. Leastwise, I read three of Conan Doyle's books on Spiritualism: *The New Revelation* (1918), *Life After Death* (1918), and *Memories and Adventures* (1924). Doyle believed in life after death. He is a creditable proponent of Spiritualism. I cannot summarily dismiss his beliefs about the spirit and our ability to communicate with it."

Can it be that our teetering atheist no longer rejects religion out of hand? Has he become a hunching agnostic, poised to take the giant leap to the Holy Spirit – God Himself?

II

<u>25 December 1925</u>.

We must have resembled smartly attired monks as we slowly walked to Westminster Abbey. The morning was chilly and a little wet, but our woolen suits and hats didn't care.

With hats removed, we entered the lordly Gothic edifice, a stone's throw from the Thames and spitting distance from the Palace of Westminster.[64]

---

[64] The Palace of Westminster is the site of the House of Commons and the House of Lords, the two chambers of the UK Parliament.

We found our way to the South Transept and Poet's Corner, the burial place of some of Britain's most accomplished poets, playwrights, and writers, including Charles John Huffam Dickens. His simple marker on the floor read:

CHARLES DICKENS
BORN 7th FEBRUARY 1812
DIED 9th JUNE 1870

Freud looked at the marker. We stood side-by-side behind him – far enough back to award him unfettered privacy at our final destination.

Forty-five minutes passed. His bent head had never moved. He looked up toward the nearby statue of Shakespeare, a sentry over Dickens's grave; turned around; and said: "I'm finished. Let's go."

I asked: "Well, what happened?"

"I'll tell everyone over lunch."

I recommended Rules in Covent Garden, two kilometres away. Our walk to the iconic restaurant was brisk and chipper.

We ordered wine and prepared to listen to Sigmund Schlomo Freud, who did not disappoint us.

"I stood at the grave and waited … and waited … and waited. At last, a spirit spoke. The inflection and accent were Queen's English. I heard the eloquent words of an educated, worldly, Victorian, middle-age man …"

Freud paused.

I pointedly asked, "What did he *say?*"

[Further lull]

"What did he *say?!*"

"Be patient, Buck. I'm thinking ... [a few more moments pass] ... His spirit said: 'My dear Sir, I have followed you and those gathered behind you continuously from Gad's Hill Place until now, as you stand, under Shakespeare's watchful eye, over my meager remains. I see the expression on your honest face. You are trying mightily to conquer disbelief as you hear the voice of a spirit. You remind me of Scrooge![65] Ha Ha Ha!'

"At that point, I had to self-confess: *Conan Doyle was right. Our spirits are within us.* Then, the spirit of the man whose trail we had followed all the way to Westminster Abbey said: 'Dr. Freud, you are a scientist, an empiricist. As well, you are a philosopher, one who draws conclusions based partly on pure deduction. You don't shun imagination. But, my friend, deduction and imagination minus *faith* are

---

[65] Note 56, supra. Ebenezer Scrooge is the protagonist in *A Christmas Carol*, which essentially is about redemption.

Scrooge, the cold-hearted miser, meets the three ghosts of Christmas, is touched by the Christmas spirit, and becomes a chivalrous, generous soul.

impotent. You *must* pay homage to faith, the highest form of human thought.

'When my bookcase at Gad's Hill grabbed your attention, I *knew* you would find the card with the code. And, *you*, Sir, *knew* you would solve the *Mysteries of Edwin Drood*. You rode your deductions, your imagination, and, yes, your *faith* to the final solution.'[66] You stepped out of Haywood Jr.'s dream and led him to the discovery of his true past.'

"I asked Dickens: 'What do you want us to do with our findings?' I waited for a few minutes and wondered: 'Is the spirit gone?'

"Finally, he spoke: 'I think faith has come upon you and Mr. Lewis. You and your fellow pilgrims are all men of integrity; distinction; discretion; and, now, *faith*. Do with your findings what The Governor of the Universe says you must do.'

"Then, there was the sound of music … inspiring music bringing vibrant peace and perfect order to my muddled mind. After it ended, I asked the man beneath our feet: 'Handel's Messiah'?[67]

"'Yes,' he said. 'It's the melody of redemption, a paean to Christ. Parts of it were played on the organ in Rochester Cathedral on

---

[66] Dickens's innocent (at that time) words, 'the final solution', bring to mind The Final Solution (1942) – the unspeakable, iniquitous Nazi plan for the genocide of Jews during World War II (1939-1945). Freud and some of his immediate family fled Vienna in 1938 to escape probable execution in Hitler's death camps. Four of his five sisters became victims of The Final Solution.

[67] George Frideric Handel (1685-1759), the acclaimed 18th-century German-born, English composer, gave the West *Messiah* (1741), his opus on the Life of Jesus, the Great Redeemer.

29 August 1861 at the funeral of Neville Walmsley, initially John Jasper.

'I kiddingly said you remind me of Scrooge. In a way, you do, Dr. Freud. Recall what he said as he awoke on Christmas morning, when he, like Neville Walmsley, realized he could atone for his past inhumanity:

> I will honour Christmas in my heart and try to keep it all the year. I will live in the Past, the Present, and the Future. The Spirits of all Three shall strive within me. I will not shut out the lessons they teach. Oh, tell me I may sponge away the writing in this stone!

'Even an atheist must admit: *some things are absolutely right, and other things are unconditionally wrong*,[68] the basic moral tenet embedded in your superego construct. He is compelled to acknowledge its origin – an Omnipotent Influence that touches all of humankind.

'Listen to Scrooge. Don't shut out the lessons the Spirits teach. Now, my friend, I bid you goodbye, but not farewell.'"[69]

"How can you remember word-for-word what Dickens said to you?"

---

[68] Notes 3 and 15, supra. C. S. Lewis, would advance this basic truth in his most significant piece of non-fiction, a collection of lectures under the title: *The Abolition of Man* (1943).

[69] 'Farewell' implies that one will never see the other person again.

"There is but one explanation, C. S. The Omnipotent Influence engrained the words into my soul."

C. S. sat upright and (reprimanding himself) said: "Well, the 'Influence' just implanted them into *my* obdurate mind.[70] Yes, even he who shuns religion, but is intellectually honest, must embrace objective value. Some things are inarguably true, and others self-evidently false. There are universal truths, like the Ten Commandments; and there are universal fallacies, like the delusional claim that 'everything is relative.'"

---

[70] The seed for *The Abolition of Man*, note 68, supra, was planted in London at Rules on 25 December 1925.

CHAPTER 12

EGYPT AND KING COTTON

[This chapter is devoted to my first grandson,
Jon Alan Gegenheimer III. His nickname: 'Jack'.]

We believe that earnest and dispassionate inquiry
amongst men experienced in all the details of the
question would lead eventually to a performance by
America of the moral duty of emancipation in a way
that might wipe out every reproach for the past
treatment of the negroes, and reflect eternal honour on
the Stars and Stripes.

Charles Dickens
Household Words
1852[71]

<u>26 December 1925</u>.

I

The early evening train to Oxford was nearly vacant. We sat in
the otherwise empty lead car. Freud sat at the window, directly across
from me and beside C. S. To my right was Professor Haywood Townes

---

[71] The quotation reflects Dickens's aversion to slavery, as he had witnessed it on his
first American visit in 1842.

183

Chambers Jr., who I still could not believe was the direct descendent of Edwin Drood.

The man who had dug up all the secrets in and around Rochester stared intently at his clasped hands as they rested on his lap.

"Sig, are you meditating?"

"We missed something, Buck."

What did we miss?"

"Egypt."

"Egypt?"

"Yes, the oppressive kingdom in *The Book of Exodus*. God helped the Israelites escape slavery there. They had been captive for 400 years before He summoned Moses to rescue them from bondage at the hands of the pharaoh and lead them to the Promised Land, the place called Canaan.[72]

"Edwin Drood was heir to his father's construction business in Egypt. On his twenty-first birthday, he was to settle there with his future wife, Rosa Bud. They had been committed to each other by agreement between their fathers. Stated differently, their marriage and life together in that faraway place would have been *involuntary*.

"Dickens's choice of Egypt as the proposed domicile of Edwin and Rosa Drood was not random. Just as biblical Egypt was a place of captivity, so was Drood's Egypt, where he was to spend the rest of his life in a forced marriage. He is pulled from the clutches of that distant

---

[72] The area comprising (a) the land between the River Jordan and the Mediterranean Sea, (b) much of today's Lebanon and Jordan, and (c) portions of western Syria.

place, which had held hostage over 600,000 Jews, when Grewgious reproves him: 'You mustn't make a plaything of a treasure!' At this point, Edwin's conscience surfaces. He will end his indelicate engagement to Rosa. Even so, he will not hold the moral compass until Crisparkle/Cleary, the Christ figure, hands it to him in the attic in #3 Minor Canon Row, after he, as Haywood Townes Chambers, completes his penitent painting of his former girlfriend, then revealed as Anne Darwin. Only then does he escape yet another kind of slavery – mental anguish born of shame. Haywood, your father was at peace when he died. That salvatory work of art cleansed his soul.

"Jasper and Princess Puffer are slaves to inner demons spawned by opium, the figurative pharaoh. Jasper, by then revealed as Walmsley, is delivered from servility to redemption, as evidenced by his suicide note. Puffer is another matter. If she sought and found salvation before she died, she, Theresa Cotton, walked hand in hand with Walmsley up the winding road to Heaven.

"Jasper, a 'slave' himself, is Rosa's master. Recall the incident early on, when Rosa is singing as Jasper accompanies her on piano. She melts down and says, 'He terrifies me ... he has made a slave of me.' For the longest time, Jasper has Rosa under his thumb, until she musters the courage to repulse him during their face-off in the Nuns' House.

"The Landless twins are literal slaves, held captive, beaten, and hounded by their inhumane stepfather. Notice how Dickens images them: 'beautiful, [innocent] barbaric [primitive] captives brought from wild tropical dominion'. That must be how he pictured the African slaves as they reached America – human cargo scooped up by transatlantic slave traders from the tropical wilderness of the Dark Continent.

"All of the tormented souls, with the probable exception of Puffer, find inner peace in the old cathedral town so near and dear to Dickens's heart. It speaks out to everyone who enters its gates: 'Sin is not welcome here!' The little 'speck on the globe' is, at first glance, dismal and confining. Its stark buildings conceal the saintly aura beneath their grey patina, just as Westminster Abbey shields the spirit of Dickens. Rochester symbolizes freedom – from slavery in all its casts. It is a place where caterpillars become butterflies, flapping their way to Heaven.

"Rochester and Gad's Hill were Dickens's Promised Land – asylum from the perils of Egypt-like London. As an aspiring youth, he fell in love with Gad's Hill Place and yearned to live, write, and prosper there. All that came to pass.

"Yes, Egypt – the clue I missed. I didn't peel back the *Drood* onion far enough. And so, I failed to reach its deepest layer."

Haywood consoled our apologetic mentor.

"Sig, your focus was on *solving the mystery*. Egypt aside, you succeeded in bringing to light what no one ever had come close to seeing. If anyone is at fault for missing the veiled slavery issue, it is *I*, the reputed Dickens expert. *I* should have peeled the onion back all the way.

"Remember what you explained about Puffer and Datchery. You didn't add them to your non-Euclidian schema because, as you said, 'they are immaterial to the solution.' The same holds true for Egypt."

"Thank you, Woody. You remind me of the magnanimous person your father turned out to be."

C. S.: "Haywood, why was Dickens so subtle in weaving slavery into the story's fabric?"[73]

"Your question merits a detailed analysis, C. S. Here goes.

"Dickens first visited America in 1842, at the rather green age of 30. He toured for five months. On the subject of the relatively new country, he was, politely stated, naive. He expected to find a beacon of freedom that would expose British societal failures. He had rightly seen the still developing nation as a noble experiment in tethered democracy – a constitutional republic set up by Enlightenment Framers who understood that government by a wild, unthinking majority necessarily leads to lawlessness and despotism, the virulent conditions that defined the French Revolution, a disastrous, godless affair that Dickens feared would befall Victorian Britain.[74] He believed that the American Revolution (1776-1781) was about the unalienable right to the pursuit of freedom guaranteed to *everyone* by the Creator.

"There was, and still is, a stain on America's image – a scarlet 'S', slavery, the so-called original sin that could burden it forever. Slavery – the calamitous institution that Britain had abolished in 1833, but which persevered in America until 1865 – hit Dickens in the face in

---

[73] Egypt is mentioned only in passing when Rosa (*Drood*, Chapter 3) snarkily asks Edwin: "And this most sensible of creatures likes the idea of being carried off to Egypt; does she, Eddy?"

[74] His anxiety about death, destruction, mob rule, and evil – so pervasive in the French Revolution (1789-1799) – prompted Dickens to write his timeless historical novel, *A Tale of Two Cities* (1859), note 13, supra.

Richmond, Virginia. His antagonism towards that miserable human predicament, wherever it existed, had always been profound. What he saw in Richmond – the treatment of men, women, and children as chattel – repulsed him. However, the perceptive visitor from London saw the wretched condition not exclusively as a Southern construct. I recall what he wrote as he took the North to task in 1861:

> Any reasonable creature may know, if willing, that the North hates the Negro and that, until it is willing to make a pretence that sympathy with him was the cause of the [Civil War], it hated the abolitionists ...[75] For the rest, there is not a pin to choose between [North and South]. They will both rant and lie and fight until they come to a compromise; and the slave will be thrown out of it, just as it happens.[76]

"Before and after the American Civil War broke out, Dickens saw moral transgression on *both* sides. He was perhaps more roused by the industrial North's rank hypocrisy than by the agrarian South's

---

[75] The Northern banking and textile industries benefited handsomely from low-cost, high-quality cotton from Southern plantations. The North was by no means willing to forego the enormous profits generated by affordable cotton, the work product of the plantation slaves who picked and harvested it.

[76] Dickens's first experience across the Atlantic is documented in *American Notes* (1842), written nineteen years before this quoted passage.

defence of its lifeblood, the plantations – where the all-important slaves worked the cotton, sugar cane, indigo, and tobacco fields. All that said, we can agree that slavery is morally indefensible."

C. S. knew the ins and outs of the war. Before Haywood could finally address his query about Dickens's 'subtle' allusion to slavery in *Drood*, the future great moral philosopher intervened.

"Woody, I'm impressed by your knowledge of slavery's role in antebellum America. May I register my thoughts before you take us to your conclusion about *Drood's* slavery theme?"

"Go ahead, C. S."

"Thank you. Bear with me.

"As you indicated, Haywood, the South's economy, its way of life, and its very culture depended chiefly on 'King Cotton'. But for slave labour, the soft, airy fibre would have died, helpless and worthless, on its stem; and the North's textile mills would have lost considerable profits. Slave labour, therefore, was almost as crucial to the North as it was to the South. When slavery was at last condemned as a deep sin, the North was *disgraced* into opposing it and going to war on account of it.

"The gory conflict, which dragged on for four torturous years (1861-1865), threw a blinding light on the bewildering American paradox: Although its founding document, the Declaration of Independence (1776) cried out that '... all men are created equal ... endowed by their Creator with certain unalienable rights [including] Life, Liberty, and the pursuit of Happiness,' it's Constitution (1789) did not expressly prohibit slavery until the interminable fighting ended with the South's surrender.[77] The disconnect between the Declaration and the Constitution dismayed Dickens, who could not reconcile America's commitment to universal freedom with its subjugation of a specific class.

"Young Dickens was considered by British law as his father's property – a child who had no real childhood ... in a very true sense, a slave. His recollection of his formative experience at the Blacking Factory aggravated his repulsion for what he had seen in Richmond.

[A pregnant pause by C. S. ... Then, a sudden exclamation]

"Flash! It has come to me! Let me think.

[A further pause]

"To convince the pharaoh to free the Jewish slaves of Egypt, God released upon that cruel nation ten plagues: Water became blood; the land was overrun by frogs and locusts; cattle died; bright, early daylight turned to sudden darkness that lasted three days; and so on. It wasn't until the tenth and final plague that the pharaoh relented. Number 10 was the worst holy curse by far: Every Egyptian family with a firstborn son would see him die by God's hand. Not one Israelite child would perish. God had directed each of His chosen ones to kill a sheep or goat and smear some of its blood above their doors. The angel from Heaven dropped the plague on all the houses except those marked with blood.

---

[77] Ratified in 1865, the Thirteenth Amendment to the U.S. Constitution abolished slavery and involuntary servitude, except as imprisonment for a crime.

"*Here's* what I *just* figured out: The Civil War was the tenth plague redux! Slavery ended only after the deaths of over 600,000 men and boys – sheep sent to great battlefields, stages for sacrifice. Just as it had taken the final *Exodus* plague to free the Israelites, it took the pestilence of internecine war to liberate the American slaves and thus fulfill the promise of the Declaration of Independence. It seems cruel, even profane, to say that the epic American conflict was God's doing. But, I don't see how any truly religious person can disagree with that notion."

Well! C.S. *is about to grab hold of religion!*

He went on.

"Dickens must have had in mind the Civil War and the end to slavery as he framed his farewell story. Much like the Israelites in Egypt and the slaves in America, the *Drood* characters found freedom at the hands of God's agent, Reverend Septimus Crisparkle – Reverend Joseph Cleary. One can argue that America's Crisparkle was Abraham Lincoln, its sixteenth president, who led the North to victory and preserved the Union. Lincoln's Emancipation Proclamation saved the republic by pulling out the roots that nourished the horrific struggle."[78]

Haywood: "Thank you for that keen analysis, C.S. Now, I shall state why, I think, Dickens was 'subtle' about slavery in *Drood*. 'Subtle' is perhaps too harsh a word here. He didn't intend to *hide* the issue. Instead, he wanted to call attention to the morbid practice whilst not

---

[78] Lincoln issued the Emancipation Proclamation on 22 September 1862, during the early stages of the Civil War. More than 3.5 million slaves (the total slave population) were deemed free persons upon their escape from the Confederacy across Union lines.

demonising those who supported its gradual, as opposed to immediate, abolition.

"There are other, deeper reasons for his knocking softly at slavery's door."

Haywood collected his thoughts.

"The overriding motive behind Dickens's scathing critique of American society and culture is expressed in his terse declaration after his 1842 visit: 'This is not the Republic I came to see. This is not the Republic of my imagination.' As C. S. aptly stated, America had conjured memories of his 'enslavement' in Warren's Blacking Factory – that period of his deprived childhood when he was forced by his parents, at age 12, to work and support his family after his spendthrift father was sent to debtors' prison. He saw his parents as 'enslavers' who had sentenced him to involuntary, child-labour servitude, a creature of the Victorian Industrial Revolution, whose culture and practices he continually excoriated in his writings.

"In 1867, Dickens returned to America. The dust of the Civil War had settled. He saw positive changes in the reunited republic, first and foremost, the abolition of slavery soon after the war ended. His attitude toward the reformed host country mellowed quite a bit. *That*, more than anything, is why slavery is a quiet *Drood* theme. Just before beginning his last story, Dickens exonerated the country that had reclaimed itself via the Thirteenth Amendment.[79]

----

[79] Note 77, supra. The Thirteenth Amendment to the U. S. Constitution (1865): "Neither slavery nor involuntary servitude, except as punishment for a crime whereof

"So, Dickens decided to 'cut America some slack'. Over and above that, the man-turned-spirit at Westminster Abbey forgave his parents for committing him to the Blacking Factory well before he began *Edwin Drood*. He felt he had to remind his readers of slavery's violation of the Golden Rule whilst not throwing mud in the faces of America, a basically good place, and of his parents, who begot him.

"Slavery brings to mind an obscured *Drood* metaphor: Before Grewgious pricked his conscience, young Edwin Drood was rakish, slavery-addicted, antebellum America. After the staid guardian of Rosa Bud scolded him for treating Rosa as his personal property, the post-adolescent fellow became the enlightened, post-bellum republic that had banished slavery and no longer treated the underclass as chattel. Redeemed Edwin Drood is redeemed America writ small."

Freud smiled at the man we had come to call 'Woody'.

"By George, I think you've got it, Woody!"[80] Or, shall I say, 'You're on the money!'[81]

Everyone laughed at the quick-witted references to *Pygmalion* and the idiom taught to Freud by William James. The welcome levity resurrected our leader's good spirits.

---

the party shall have been duly convicted, shall exist within the United States, or any place subject to its jurisdiction."

[80] Freud had seen George Bernard Shaw's *Pygmalion* in Vienna, where it was produced in German in 1913. Among its many catchy lines is the spirited declaration by Professor Henry Higgins: "By George, I think she's got it!" – referring to Eliza Doolittle's long-sought and successful command of prim and proper King's English.

[81] Note 24, supra.

II

As we disembarked at Oxford Station, I noticed C. S.'s pensive mood.

"C. S., what, may I ask, are you up to?"

"I'm going to make a phone call."

He who would become the 20th century's most respected moral philosopher and Christian apologist entered the red phone box a few metres away. As he talked and listened, I fidgeted. He spent ten minutes on the phone. When he hung up, I asked, "What's going on?"

"Buck, you're such a Nervous Nellie."

"Why do you punish me with *that* name?"

"Because you *act* like Nervous Nellie."

"Well, Nervous Nellie is famished!"

"So am I. I'm sure Sig and Woody are, as well. *That's* why I made the phone call. I just booked our dinner at the Randolph, in the same room where our momentous journey began. You all will like the meal. I promise!"

The familiar hotel was a welcome sight. C. S. had booked two double rooms, one for Freud and him and the other for Haywood and me – the same arrangements we had enjoyed in Rochester. We would have a late dinner before bed.

C. S.: "The chef said it would take him and the staff about ninety minutes to prepare dinner. I propose we jaunt down to the Eagle & Child and relax over a pint or two."

The fun-loving Irishman was fond of Guinness, the dark stout of St. James Gate, Dublin. He ordered four straightaway. We were not offended. We knew that the sincere teaching fellow was not being impolite. He simply wanted us to share his Platonic enjoyment of the hearty brew.

We talked mostly about religion and how our Rochester/London excursion had influenced our attitudes about the Deity. Haywood and I always had been committed Christians. Our time with Dickens and *Drood* reinforced our religious conviction. It materially changed C. S.'s attitude about faith. He conceded to the empirical evidence that had emanated from Dickens's grave. But to him, the concept of a personal God was still dubious.

A mere colleague and acquaintance to Haywood and me a fortnight ago, C. S. Lewis was now our dear friend, the person whom we would call, from 26 December 1925 forward, 'Jack'.[82] After Rochester, Jack, Haywood, I, and other academics (we dubbed ourselves 'the Inklings') often explored the idea of faith on Thursday evenings at the Eagle & Child. At the early stage of his rich, eventful adulthood, no one suspected that C. S. Lewis, the hesitant atheist, would become a devoted Christian and go on to write some of the most influential moral/theological works of his time.[83] I am convinced that

____

[82] Note 3, supra.

[83] Note 68, supra.

Gad's Hill, Rochester, Westminster Abbey, and the urgings of Tolkien five years later,[84] led him to Christianity.

Freud is another matter. Before 1925, he unreservedly belittled religion. His Great Awakening began with our dreamlike adventure of 11-25 December 1925. His personal contact with a spirit and with phenomena that defy scientific explanation pulled him toward belief in the supernatural. By 25 December 1925, Sigismund Schlomo Freud could no longer categorically deny the existence of Something or Someone outside the human domain. Dickens's words to him at the Abbey – "You must pay homage to faith, the highest form of human introspection ..." were forever etched in his mind.

Before we left the Eagle & Child, I asked C. S. and Freud how the last fourteen days had affected their religious leanings. Their joint response: "We cannot deny offhand the existence of a sole, all-powerful Influence. If It, He, or She is mere fantasy, we are nothing more than self-conscious, spiritless flesh. So says the spirit of Dickens."

[Years later, something would happen to Freud. His last book, *Moses and Monotheism* (1939), casts a negative light on Moses. There, he claims that the biblical man he came to respect in the closing days of 1925 had led only his close friends and followers out of Egypt. He further asserts that religion in general is a symptom of neurosis. I was crestfallen as I read his assaultive indictments of faith. I struggled to figure out my famous friend's baffling regression and finally concluded: *Perhaps the escalating Nazi persecution of Jews in 1938, which*

---

[84] Note 15, supra.

presaged the Holocaust (1941-1945), gave him pause. He must have sensed the inevitability of Jewish genocide at the hands of the Nazis and lost the faith that he had gained in Rochester and Westminster Abbey.

As it turned out, Freud would re-embrace religion shortly after he wrote that last book. His 1939 letter to me, written shortly after the outbreak of World War II in Europe,[85] is his mea culpa. It is much more, however. That heartwarming correspondence was a precursor to something he would send to me to pass on to Buck Jr. It is in my attic for my son to discover.]

III

[Back to 26 December 1925]

Expecting us at the Randolph was the same lonesome table in the same reclusive room we had occupied on the evening of 10 December. Two carafes of rosy wine and four round, stemless glasses sat on an oval tray atop a small sideboard standing at attention against the near wall.

The waiter appeared with a basket of flat, kibbled bread. Freud, the secular but scholarly Jew, figured out what C. S. had orchestrated from the train station's phone box.

---

[85] The 5 September 1939 letter hopefully will be discovered by my son.

"Aaah! C. S., you thoughtfully designed for us a Seder meal to commemorate the Israelites' Augean[86] journey from slavery to freedom in the Promised Land.

"This unleavened bread stands for matzah, which the *Haggadah*[87] calls 'the bread of affliction'. The endangered Israelites had to flee Egypt before the bread could rise.

"The Seder is one of the very few Jewish ceremonies that, regardless of my antipathy towards religion, I have observed. I have read from the *Haggadah*. I am fluent in Hebrew. My wife knows the text by heart.

"The wine symbolises freedom from servitude. Each of us shall drink four glasses. When God pledged to lead the Jews to freedom, he stressed four words: (a) 'I shall *take* you out'; (b) 'I shall *rescue* you'; (c) 'I shall *redeem* you ...'; (d) 'I shall *bring* you ...'[88] There are other reasons for drinking four cups of wine. Let those I just stated suffice for now."

The waiter set down four small saucers of horseradish and a pasty spread of dates and walnuts.

Freud: "The horseradish substitutes for the pungent herbs eaten to remind us of the atrocities endured by the Israelite slaves. The fruit-

---

[86] The adjective is based on Augeas, the mythical Greek king whose stables housed thousands of cattle. Heracles (Hercules in Latin) was given the arduous, seemingly impossible task of removing the massive quantity of dung from the stables. He succeeded by rerouting two rivers to wash away the filth. 'Augean' has come to mean 'of unusual difficulty'. It is synonymous with 'Herculean'.

[87] The text cited at Seder on the first and second nights of Passover. It includes all of *Exodus*.

[88] *Exodus*, 6:6-8.

and-nut spread is charoset – meant to resemble the clay they used to make bricks.

"C. S., how are you, an Oxford agnostic, so familiar with the Seder?"

"Like you, Professor Freud, I have not been a person of faith. I have, however, studied religion: Judaism, Christianity, and even Islam. I see this lovely repast as a good way to celebrate what Woody has shared with us concerning Dickens's restrained slap at slavery."

Freud: "Now, what did you order for the remaining courses?"

"In order of presentation, we shall enjoy matzah ball soup; poached salmon salad with beets; and brisket, potato casserole, and carrot-and-prune stew. For dessert, there's Passover chocolate torte with strawberries, and strong coffee."

"Wunderbar! More popular Seder foods! Each symbolic item has its purpose. I can't wait!"

Dinner was splendid. As we finished coffee and dessert, C. S. stood:

"Woody and Buck, this dinner was for *you*, as well. Christians have their own version of the Passover meal as a re-creation of the Last Supper, when Christ instituted the Eucharist.[89] The Christian Seder features much of the same food and drink offered by its *Old Testament* ancestor."

---

[89] The Christian rite (sacrament), also called Holy Communion, commemorating the Last Supper, when Christ consecrated the bread and wine as his body and blood.

The seeming presumptuousness of Clive Staples 'Jack' Lewis was not presumptuousness at all. Our loving friend simply wanted us to know that Freud and he had come to accept religion's place in the affairs of men.

As I write the final words of this one-of-a-kind story, Einstein and Freud come to mind. Einstein famously said: "Science without religion is lame; religion without science is blind."[90] The reader will recall what my friends Freud and C. S. said earlier in these pages: "We cannot deny offhand the existence of 'God'. If It, He, or She is mere fantasy, we are nothing more than self-conscious, spiritless flesh …"

If Einstein – the beyond-compare scientific savant with a boundless imagination, he who sought and found the inconceivable Fourth Dimension,[91] recognises the symbiotic relationship between science and religion; and my learned colleagues, men of philosophy and science, came to realise that faith and empiricism are partners, how can *anyone* out-and-out deny the existence of God or, for that matter, discount the legitimacy of science?

Chiswell Bucktrout Sr.
1 July 1981
A*M*D*G

---

[90] From Einstein's essay, "Science and Religion" (1954).

[91] Einstein identified 'space-time' as the Fourth Dimension, something far removed from the earthbound limits of the other three: height, width, and depth.

EPILOGUE
"SPIRITS IN THE SKY"

When I die and they lay me to rest

Gonna go to the place that's the best …

Goin' up to the spirit in the sky …

I got a friend in Jesus

So you know that when I die …

He's gonna set me up with

The spirit in the sky

Norman Greenbaum
"Spirit in the Sky"
1969[92]

I

I am Chiswell Bucktrout Jr., born 9 December 1933. I am a stubbornly fit and alert nonagenarian, approaching age 92. Like my father was, I am an only child. My proud nickname: 'Buck'. I retired as a professor of English Literature at Magdalen College, Oxford in 1998. Since 1983, I have owned the preceding manuscript – my father's moving narration of that glorious two-week emprise born at the Randolph Hotel in Beaumont Street, Oxford and consummated at that same claustral place.

Chiswell Bucktrout Sr. died on 11 July 1983. A ribbon-wrapped package was at his bedside. He guided my hand to it as he

---

[92] "Spirit in the Sky" is an 'oddly compelling' amalgam of gospel and hard rock music. The lyrics suggest Norman Greenbaum's belief in Spiritualism.

passed away. Taped to it was his folded message: "Buck, open this package soon after I am gone. Forever, Your Loving Father – on this 5th day of July, 1983. A*M*D*G"

I went home after his touching memorial service on 15 July and opened the package. A touching letter, which I have kept and cherished, was paper-clipped to the cover page bearing the enclosed manuscript's title – *The Canon Code*.

4 July 1983

My dear Buck,

Two years ago, I completed this manuscript, which lay in my attic safe until now.

You and I passed many evenings at the Eagle & Child discussing *The Mystery of Edwin Drood*. Yet, we never talked about what follows: guarded secrets that have been preserved for a long time.

I was part of a four-man delegation sent by God on 11 December 1925 to solve the *Drood* mystery. With me were Sigmund Freud, C. S. Lewis, and Professor Haywood Chambers Jr. You knew Professors Lewis and

Chambers and respected them very much. As you will recall, Professor Lewis died in 1963, and Professor Chambers passed away in 1944. Dr. Freud left us in 1939, when you were just shy of six. He was quite a man. I'm sorry you never met him.

In 1932, over dinner at Rules, they appointed me to write *The Canon Code* 'whenever Something (or Someone) tells me it is time.'

When you were born, God told us *you* should broadcast Dickens's clever plan by publishing this manuscript.

You'll soon follow the sacred road travelled by two 27-year-old teaching fellows; Professor Chambers, whose true identity will astound you; and the Founder of Psychoanalysis – as they hunt for literature's Holy Grail. Read the manuscript before you dine in the quiet side-room at the Randolph, your first waypoint.

Cherish every moment of 10 December to 26 December 1925. Then, after God clears the way, deliver the manuscript to the Oxford University Press.

Well, it's time to say goodbye. We shall meet again, after you finish your calling on Earth, if not before then. Godspeed, my son.

Love,

Dad

A*M*D*G

[Two golden keys were firmly taped to the letter.]

II

For three days, I was amazed by what I had read. Beginning on 18 July 1983, I followed the trail left fifty-eight years earlier by four purposeful men – from their solitary dinner at the Randolph, where I enjoyed the same meal they had savoured; to Gad's Hill School; to Rochester and the weir, the cave, the cathedral, and #3 Minor Canon Row; and to London and Westminster Abbey.

On 24 July, I entered the venerated church sheltering the remains of Dickens. In Poet's Corner, at the grave below the sentient eye of Shakespeare, a spectral voice commanded: "Buck Jr., take the keys; go to the attic; and open the wardrobe."

I managed to respond: "Is that you, Mr. Dickens?"

"Yes. It is I."

"Mr. Dickens, are you alone?"

"No, Buck Jr. I am standing beside someone who loves you."

"Buck, listen to our dear friend. Use the keys and open the wardrobe."

That voice was all too familiar.

"I'll use the keys, Dad. I won't let you down. Are Dr. Freud, Professor Lewis, and Professor Chambers also there?"

"They're standing behind Mr. Dickens and me, as they adoringly smile down at you.

"Buck, one more thing, a reminder."

"What, Dad?"

"Wait for God's instruction. Goodbye, Buck. Happy trails, until we meet again."[93]

I responded in a quivering voice: "I'll listen every day for His Word. Goodbye to each of you. Happy trails to my spirits in the sky. I love you all."

Peering through teary eyes, I walked to Rules.

---

[93] My dad and I listened to and watched on UK radio and television the 1940s and 1950s American Western starring Roy Rogers and Dale Evans. "Happy Trails" was the theme song for that popular programme. The sentimental lyrics, written by Evans, was sung by the famous duo at the conclusion of each episode. Its familiar opening and closing lines: "Happy trails to you, until ('til) we meet again."

<u>25 July 1983</u>.

III

Back in Oxford, I entered the Bucktrout house on Main Street and climbed the stairs to the attic. I had never been in that out-of-sight room until that day. The golden keys rested safely in my trousers pocket. They were the same size and had solid, disk-shaped bows, one marked with the letter A and the other with W. I used A to open the garret door. A modest, yet noticeable crystal chandelier hung at the centre of the dim room. The light switch was about fifteen centimetres to my left. I pushed up the switch. The potent chandelier glared, and the whole room came into focus.

A regal wardrobe stood triumphantly at the far wall. The imposing fixture seemed to breathe as it absorbed much of the light thrown its way. C. S. Lewis's *The Chronicles of Narnia*: *The Lion, the Witch, and the Wardrobe*[94] came to mind:

Four children in World War II London are evacuated to a manor house, far away from the Nazi Blitzkrieg. Lucy, the youngest, explores the house and comes upon an enormous wardrobe – the gateway to a snow-covered land called Narnia, a sad place where it is 'always winter, but never Christmas'. Lucy sees much of Narnia and meets a few engaging inhabitants, who tell her much about it. She finds

---

[94] *The Lion, the Witch, and the Wardrobe* (1950) is the first of seven novels in a series set in the fictional place called Narnia. A lion, killed by a witch's spell, rises from the dead. The lion symbolizes Christ.

her way back home and reveals to her siblings everything she discovered in the strange, snow-covered land light years past the wardrobe. They don't believe her, until they follow her through the wardrobe to Narnia, which they learn is a kingdom under the spell of an evil witch. The four London child-heroes, helped by a lion who had overcome death, banish the witch and become Narnia's rulers.

I did not have to guess where the wardrobe in the attic of the Bucktrout house would take *me*. A small bronze plaque was mounted at the centre of its tall, wide door:

> This armoire, the way to the true world of Edwin Drood, is left (with all of its contents) on this 31st day of July in the year of our Lord 1926 to Sigmund S. Freud, who answered Western literature's most abiding question: What happened to Edwin Drood?
>
> Rt. Rev. Jeremy Roundtree
> Dean of Rochester

How did the wardrobe find its way here?

I inserted W into the ready and willing keyhole, turned him clockwise, and opened the door. *Déjà vu!* Hanging on a single rack extending from side to side were a coat and its complementary trousers, vest, shirt, and cravat. They looked sad, as did the pair of dry, wrinkled, brown leather shoes, with silty socks, minding their business on the wardrobe's floor. A tatty painting of the girl who must be Anne Darwin

(Rosa Bud) hung on the rear wall. Single shelves mounted to my left and right held boxes identical to those described in my father's manuscript. Something else drew my attention: an unsealed, sky-blue envelope beneath a crystal paperweight that emitted luring, blue rays:

Sigmund S. Freud, MD
20 Maresfield Gardens
London
England

Professor Chiswell Bucktrout
Magdalene College
High Street
Oxford
England

I opened the envelope and read Freud's note, neatly hand-written in blue ink on white paper:

5 September 1939
14:00

Dear Buck,

Earlier today, I shipped to you from my London residence the wardrobe and its contents, left to me by Jeremy Roundtree. I had managed to smuggle everything out of Vienna just before I fled for London, last year. You can re-place the contents in their original spots – in that grand piece of furniture from #3 that led us, step by step, to what happened to Edwin Drood.

Buck, *you* should have the wardrobe. Preserve it for your son, whom the Almighty chose to reveal Dickens's finished story to humankind.

Before I close, I must explain something about which you must be surprised and disappointed: what I wrote in *Moses and Monotheism*. You and the others must have thought: *What happened to Sig? He trashed religion and took back everything he said to us during that beautiful fortnight in December 1925.*

When the Nazis burned my books and began the systematic persecution and execution of innocent Jews, I lost the faith I had gained. Somehow, just after the publication of my acerbic treatise, I took my second leap to belief in the Almighty. I had thought about Churchill: *He will conquer and lay waste to Hitler and his thugs. The great Briton must have been sent by God.*

A wise man someday will write:

"The essence of faith lies in the process

of searching for it. True faith includes

doubt and embraces wonder."[95]

I tried unsuccessfully to recall the

book from the publisher. The bell had

already been rung. I couldn't 'unring' it.

Can you, C. S., and Haywood forgive me

for my regrettable diatribe?

Until we next meet,[96] God be

with you.

Ever yours,

Sig.

IV

Every Monday evening, for quite a few years, the Bucktrouts

Sr. and Jr. had sat over clarets in the Rabbit Room at the Eagle & Child.

I walked there to ponder the last few days. The bartender, a

septuagenarian whom, for forty-plus years, my father called Pip[97] (his

name was Tim Pippins), walked to my side of the bar with two glasses

---

[95] Freud's prescience is otherworldly. The quoted words would be written by Gary Saul Morsun in his article, "Fyodor Dostoevsky's Struggle with Faith", *The Wall Street Journal*, Section A, p. 13, 28 February 2025.

[96] Freud died on 23 September 1939 in London. He had advanced oral cancer and did not live to see his friend after he wrote the 5 September 1939 letter.

[97] He had in mind Philip Pirrip, called 'Pip' – the protagonist/narrator in Dickens's *Great Expectations* (1861).

of Moses Montefiore claret. He set one before me and the other to my right, at the place Buck Sr. always had sat. Then, he handed me a brown envelope, written in letter-perfect script: 'Chiswell Bucktrout Jr.'

"Buck, your dad was here on 9 July. He was so frail. The walk here must have been an ordeal – like Christ's walk up the Via Dolorosa. He handed me this envelope and said: 'Buck will be here in a few days, by himself. Give him this and be sure he opens it here, where the Inklings[98] gathered every Thursday evening and he and I bonded every Monday before dinner for so many years.'

"Well, Buck, go ahead and see what's in the envelope."

It was tightly sealed. Dependable Pip handed me a letter opener. I carefully pulled out an oversized, timeworn card, protected by laminate, with garbled words (except for DROOD) and a set of apparent initials – in faded black letters:

DROOD ... NACON ... TICTA ... NEAD

C. J. H. D.

There were two other items – old, laminated newspaper clippings:

---

[98] Notes 68 and 83, supra. The Inklings, mentioned earlier by my father, were a close Oxford fellowship that met weekly in the Rabbit Room at the Eagle & Child. The membership, consisting of twenty or so scholars, included C. S. Lewis, J. R. R. Tolkien, Haywood Chambers Jr., and Chiswell Bucktrout Sr. The group met for nearly two decades between the early 1930s and late 1949. Missing for the final five years was Haywood Chambers Jr., who died in 1944.

DAILY NEWS

London, 12 September 1855

Five passengers died, and seventy-five were critically injured, yesterday – when an outbound train from London to Dover derailed ten kilometers outside London. A railway spokesman said it is a miracle that only five persons were killed outright.

Taped to the above piece was the continuation Freud had clipped off:

Neal and Indira Stanley, seated on either side of their son, Haywood Stanley, suffered gruesome, fatal traumas to their heads and necks. Haywood's uncle, Neville Walmsley, in the same cabin, sustained severe, internal damage.

Master Stanley, only 15, had been, like his parents and uncle, dreadfully battered, but his injuries were somehow only minor and superficial. Uncharacteristically composed for one so young, he stated at the scene: "Miraculously, I am alive and unharmed.

God saved me. I pray for my parents, who are in Heaven. I pray as well for my uncle's fast and full recovery."

DAILY NEWS

London, 10 June 1865

The Southeastern Railway Folkstone to London derailed where a section of track had been removed for engineering purposes. Ten were killed, and forty were injured. On the train was Charles Dickens, who tended the victims, some of whom died.

During the next week, I studied every item in the 'Narnian' wardrobe and harkened back to those halcyon days shared by four crusaders, who listened to their hearts and found #3 Minor Canon Row, home to that magnificent appurtenance and all the relics that had told the world the true essence of Dickens's last story.

V

<u>19 April 1984</u>.

It was Maundy Thursday, nearly nine months since my evening at the Eagle & Child with Pip. As I began lunch, Something (or

Someone) whispered: "Call the Randolph and make a dinner reservation for this evening."

I reached the maitre d'.

"Sir, may I reserve a place for one for dinner this evening?"

"What's your name?"

"Professor Chiswell Bucktrout Jr."

"One moment ... [a ten-second pause] ...

"Professor Bucktrout, we already have you down for dinner at 19:00. There's a notation: 'Special meal for Professor Bucktrout Jr. is prepared and ready to serve.'"

"That's strange! I didn't call."

"Well, *someone* did, Professor ... wait a second ... I see the name 'Jack' in blue script, to the side of the notation. Is there someone whom you know as 'Jack'?"

[I looked to the sky.]

"As a matter of fact, there is! I'll be sure to thank my friend for making the reservation."

I arrived at the bar a half hour before dinner and ordered a Guinness. Raising my glass to the Place Upstairs, I toasted my beloved, departed friend: "To you, my faithful buddy, whom I met when I was only five, and you just forty ... to you, my dear, presumptuous 'Jack'. You haven't changed a bit. I see you as you stand on the other side of the Rainbow Bridge ... raising *your* glass of Guinness."

The spirit of C. S. Lewis merrily rang out: "Enjoy the Holy Thursday Seder, Buck Jr. I'm always thinking of you."

I blew him a kiss, said "thank you", and took my seat at the table-for-one, situated all by itself in the nostalgic, tucked-away room reserved this time just for me. But, I wasn't by myself as I re-lived the fairy-tale night of 26 December 1925. Five spirits, Dickens included, were at my side. We talked and reminisced for the longest time. The company and the conversation were divine.

VI

<u>9 April 2020</u>.

Thirty-six years have passed since that sacramental evening. For each of those years, on Maundy Thursday, I have enjoyed the company of my 'spirits in the sky' – those great, decent men to whom we owe the 'whole truth and nothing but the truth' about *The Mystery of Edwin Drood*.

Upon arriving home from the Randolph on *this* Maundy Thursday night, 2020, I sensed that something profound soon would happen.

VII

<u>9 June 2020</u>.

On the 150th anniversary of the death of Charles Dickens, I was in the Rabbit Room, enjoying an evening Guinness and hoping to hear from Jack in the place he had made famous. Instead, there came a different voice, and orotund command that could have emanated only from Above:

215

"Hello, Buck. I am He from Heaven. The time to reveal *The Canon Code* is near. You will know when that day arrives."

He said nothing further.

For nearly thirty-seven years, I had awaited The Word from Him. He chose *now* – these troubled, politically charged, *postmodernist* times that "try men's souls"[99] – to place me on notice.

VIII

The Mystery of Edwin Drood is an unmitigated indictment of opium and the damage it caused to the moral and social fabric of Victorian England. Today, that nocuous narcotic and its most deadly derivative, fentanyl, menace much of the world, just as the plagues of pestilence, war, terrorism, and barbarity continue to blitz the global landscape and humanity's 'mindscape'. Charles Dickens deserves high acclaim for weaving the opium theme into his last and finest work and for upbraiding slavery, the plague that, since pre-biblical times, has victimized so many – of every race, creed, and ethnicity – almost everywhere.

---

[99] "These are the times that try men's souls" are the words of Thomas Paine (1737-1809) in reference to the American Revolution. His pamphlet, *Common Sense* (1775-76), advocated American independence from Great Britain.

Postmodernism is the deluded ideology that espouses moral relativism – the 'anything-goes' view that there are no objective standards of right and wrong. Postmodernism strongly influences today's social and political discourse. It is the philosophy that C. S. Lewis slammed in *The Abolition of Man*. Notes 68, 83, supra.

<u>The Very Recent Past and the Present: 2020-2025.</u>

IX

We owe Charles Dickens praise for pointing us to something else: the idea that plagues, howsoever they appear, will *always* challenge us: pandemics; worldwide conflict that brings death, devastation, and economic angst; rampant crime; violent, destructive mob protest in cities and towns and on college campuses; and so on. Lurking in the shadows is the plague that feeds all those calamities: 'postmodernism', which wreaks havoc far and wide. Riots, arson, looting, desecration of statues and houses of worship, demonisation of the police, and general mayhem – all committed, under the guise of free speech, as redress for baseless grievances – are avatars of Jacobin, Bolshevik, Marxist mob rule in bustling cities and sleepy towns, not only in America, but around the globe.

By desolating the statues of prominent historical figures, some of them controversial, the Leftist iconoclasts seek to erase the past and thus rub out history. They are fully aware that a nation bereft of its past is ripe for Marxist reformation. They follow Lenin's playbook from cover to cover, and they have found more than a few allies on the Left.

The modern-day Jacobins also seek to tear down the English language by rewriting the lexicon to change the meanings of or even discard basic, time-honoured words and phrases. A nation where words mean whatever one wants them to mean is a place that, sooner or later, will lose its freedom.

X

The *Exodus* plagues and, I am afraid, the American Civil War, were acts of God. Opium, fentanyl, terrorism, genocide, war solely for the sake of conquest, the ideological and physical invasion of college campuses, and galloping anti-Semitism – all indicia of postmodernism – are Satan's handiwork.

These are times hauntingly similar to the hellish, soulless episode that was the French Revolution, those 'worst of times' that Dickens feared would resurface in Victorian England.[100] We are witnessing the rebirth of radical, Jacobin-inspired, French Revolution-style postmodernism, the baneful metaphysic that shouts: "The end justifies the means; it's us against them!" Today's postmodernists, the culprits behind the current anarchy, do not think; they *feel*. They defecate on the moral compass. They *feel* that one may violate any tenet of the code of objective morals as recompense for the imagined or actual breach of another teaching in that same code. The avengers ignore The Golden Rule. Their hypocritical, double-standard mindset is what C.S. Lewis so eloquently and cogently runs down in *The Abolition of Man*.[101]

XI

From the High Clouds, Freud's spirit proclaims: "We live in id-dominant times. The horse threw its rider and runs wild in the

---

[100] Note 74, supra.

[101] Notes 68, 83, and 99, supra.

streets." To the anarchists, society's rules and laws are meaningless abstractions; and religion is a crutch for emotional cripples. Today's miscreants, who (a) desecrate or dismantle historical statues, monuments, and memorials; (b) ravage churches, synagogues, and mosques; and (c) undertake unwarranted foreign invasions live by the postmodernist Hitlerian-Leninist motto: "Might makes right." A heaven-sent leader, one who is, for the most part, someone of unimpeachable rectitude and Churchillian perseverance, must emerge to challenge those who, if left unchecked, will bring on economic collapse; moral decay; religious persecution; world government run by unelected, socialist bureaucrats; and other such 'plagues' that will bring humankind to its knees.

XII

Is the Prince of Darkness dancing amongst us? Are we on the fast track to tyranny? Is 2020-2025 the harbinger of *1984*?[102] Is this topsy-turvy world going to Hell in a handbasket? Are we fast approaching our darkest hour? Will the Creator send someone to deliver us from the evil that is polluting our collective soul? Is that person, the 21st-century superego, already here? Jack, the sapient moral philosopher who exposed and discredited postmodernism, knows the answers to

---

[102] *1984* (1949) is the dystopian novel by English writer George Orwell (1903-1950) that foresees government dysfunction, corruption, and Marxist overreach in a place redolent of today's America and much of the rest of the modern world.

those urgent questions. *The Screwtape Letters* comes to mind.[103] I intend to continue my reexamination of what he says there ... and elsewhere; and I shall talk about this utterly confused world, a place that has lost its way, at my Holy Thursday get-togethers with him and the others.[104]

XIII

Chiswell Bucktrout Sr. called out moral relativism, i. e., postmodernism, just as C. S. Lewis did; and just as Dickens did at Westminster Abbey on 25 December 1925, when he reproved Freud: "Even an atheist like you, Dr. Freud, must admit that some things are [objectively] right, and other things are [in the same way] wrong ... He is compelled to acknowledge [that immutable tenet's] origin – a [transcendental] Influence that touches all of humankind." That basic truth, uttered by the spirit of the 19th century's most astute observer of the human condition, rings hollow during these unprecedented times – when God is near His deathbed. We are in a tug-of-war for man's soul, which is closer to Lucifer's grasp than it has ever been. Perhaps Buck Sr.'s rare chronicle, along with my modest contribution to his effort, can

---

[103] *The Screwtape Letters* (1942) is a Christian apologetic novel in which C. S. Lewis describes human temptation and emotion from the Devil's perspective. Screwtape (the Devil) and his nephew, Wormwood, epically fail to corrupt the soul of a man who finds his way to Heaven.

[104] Ever since my Maundy Thursday dinner in the mystic room at the Randolph on 19 April 1984, I have celebrated every subsequent Holy Thursday evening alone at the same table, experiencing the Seder in the heavenly company of my father, Dr. Freud, Woody Chambers, Jack, and, of course, the great Mr. Dickens. I ask the reader: Wouldn't you love to join us and hear what we have to say?

help us repel those minatory forces that seek to destroy Western civilisation.

The Maker said I would know when to offer these pages to readers far and wide. I believe in my heart of hearts that the time *is now*, when postmodernism has the world by the throat. I hope that the next 'saviour',[105] whoever he/she might be, will find inspiration in what my beautiful father and I have imparted here.

On 11 July 2025, the forty-second anniversary of my father's death, I shall deliver *The Canon Code: Freud, C. S. Lewis, et al. Solve The Mystery of Edwin Drood*[106] to the Oxford University Press. Five sublime spirits will be at my side.

Chiswell Bucktrout Jr.
4 July 2025
A*M*D*G

---

[105] I use the lower case because I do not know that the person is divine. I *do* know that he/she carries the moral compass and will never let it go.

[106] I added the subtitle because Sigmund Freud and the great men who helped him to decipher the Canon Code should receive credit at the outset.

The reader has also seen that my considerate father furnished footnotes throughout his manuscript to lend context to this story. I decided to follow his example by furnishing my own. I hope the readers will appreciate our efforts.